INTERESTING STORIES

Deepanshu Srivastava

INDIA • SINGAPORE • MALAYSIA

ISBN 979-8-89133-684-1

Dedicated to my beloved mother
Ms Manju Srivastava

Contents

The Orchard

In Raigad, a sleepy town in the Konkan region of Maharashtra, Ajinkya Patil used to live with his mother Ushatai Patil, elder sister Sunita Patil and cousin Vandana Patil. The youngster, a dendrophile, went to US Agriculture Academy to learn more about trees and plants. After coming back he started research on different species of mango trees in a mango orchard. He also got attracted to his cousin, Vandana, and started spending his time either in the orchard or with Vandana.

His mother did not like Ajinkya getting closer to Vandana and smelled his one-sided affection towards his cousin, Vandana. To stop the blind love of her young son, she asked Vandana to go back to her father's place in Pune away from Raigad. For carrying out his research he applied for procuring funds to different agencies but in vain. Then he asked his mother for monetary help but she expressed her reluctance as she was to marry her daughter soon and her resources were limited. These two incidences affected Ajinkya mentally and with time he became a loner and eccentric after his mother's death and sister's marriage.

He soon begins to suspect that there are some people in the village who wanted to create hindrance in his research and started believing that the caretaker of the orchard Shivani, wife of his family's servant Mandar is a Goddess who so lovingly takes care of his workplace, the orchard. After a few days, his sister Sunita invited Ajinkya to her house to celebrate her husband Girish's promotion. While socialising at the party with other guests, Ajinkya started feeling uneasy in the crowd and he started behaving unusually, disrespecting the guests with foul language and unacceptable behaviour. Sunita tried to cool him down but his behaviour remained unchanged. Her husband Girish became upset due to Ajinkya's s erratic behaviour towards his invitees. A doctor in the party, after examining Ajinkya, referred him to a psychiatrist.

After coming back home, Ajinkya kept on visualising and talking about the orchard, and his so-called Goddess Shivani. Vandana also made frequent appearances in his dreams. He had disillusion that Shivani got murdered by her husband Mandar for her kindness and full involvement in the upkeep of the orchard. The treatment of the psychiatrist although took care of Ajinkya's s erratic behaviour but could not treat his fantasy and imaginary world of disillusionment. It was a difficult situation for the entire family and all of them were living under stress. Even Ajinkya used to take his medicines occasionally. Sunita asks Vandana not to meet Ajinkya anymore due to her apprehension of Ajinkya's mental conditions to get worst.

As it is said that every cloud has a silver lining, the family met a social worker, Amruta Rane who was running a care center for mental sickness. She agreed to admit Ajinkya and the center started his counseling sessions.

Ajinkya also came to understand that he has some mental issues and he needed to take responsibility for his own well-being. He decided to get rid of his mental illness with his determination and willpower. The counseling sessions, therapy given in the center, and changed the positive outlook of Ajinkya altogether took Ajinkya out of his mental sickness and he started looking towards life to achieve his goal of researching the mango species in Maharashtra. He returned back happily to Raigad with a new zeal. A piece of Good news was also waiting for Ajinkya in Raigad. Maharashtra government had accepted his application for the grant of funds to carry out his project. Learning this Ajinkya's happiness knew no bounds. The story confirms the fact that with willpower, determination, and a positive outlook a person can achieve his goal.

The Debt

Vidarbha, a north-eastern region of Maharashtra, has remained backward industrially and agriculturally. One of the various reasons is the formation of large basaltic rocks throughout Vidarbha leading to crop failure, increased cost of cultivation, and poor irrigation facilities. Consequently, about 70% of farmers–suicides are from 11 districts of this region. The living conditions of farmers are quite low as compared to the rest of Maharashtra. This story revolves around a farmer, Ashok Bhonsale who was living happily with his wife Meghana, 8-year-old son Dattatreya, and 03 acres of cultivated land in Wardha, a small and remote town of Vidarbha region. Ashok was different from his peer farmers as he was very hard-working, mentally tough, and had never–say–die approach.

The story categorically describes the way how lack of education and proper information system among most of the farmers have been ruining their lives despite their indefatigable spirit. Due to difficult situations prevailing everywhere over the last two years coupled with scanty rains and improper irrigation facilities, many farmers in this region were forced to end their lives by drinking pesticides. They were unable to repay loans mostly taken from private landlords and the banks owing to crop failure. After such a drastic step taken by Ashok's friend and fellow farmer Vinayak Rao Jadhav, Ashok also got engulfed badly by depression and suicidal thoughts. His wife Meghana notices her husband's segregated mental status and feels that Ashok is also contemplating suicide. She asks her son Dattatreya to keep a watch on Ashok and inform her of any irregular behaviour of Ashok.

On the other hand, Ashok was imbued by thoughts of the arrival of the monsoon. But it was proving to be a mirage. During these days, Meghana tried her best by preparing

"Thaleepeeths" and "Pooranpolees" among other delicacies along with a number of myriad efforts to keep Ashok in good spirits. Ashok being inherently mentally stronger than his peer farmers was often annoyed by the over-caring and misplaced concern of his wife. Ashok decides to pawn Meghana's s jewellery with her consent and purchases cotton seeds from Pune city and sowed them. However, the seeds failed to germinate due to the late arrival of the monsoons. This brought a storm in Ashok's life. Meghana observing Ashok's determination to fight the situation sold her remaining jewelry and borrowed some more money to purchase a fresh bag of seeds and they sowed them. Due to the vagaries of the rains, they could reap only two quintals of cotton. But the entire production was taken away by the money lenders who had lent money to Bhonsales for purchasing seeds and fertilisers. The Bhonsale were left with no part of the produce. Since Ashok, by nature, has been a fighter, he went to a bank in Pune and loaned rupees 03 lakhs for installing a borewell in his field.

Ashok installed the borewell despite the perpetual pessimism shown by the village sarpanch on Ashok's ideas to draw the water from his borewell. Continuing the stormy days of Ashok, his borewell also did not function to its full capacity owing to the erratic power supply (a trend which is very common to the hinterlands of Vidarbha where Wardha is located). Seeing a space to fulfill their greeds due to Ashok's conditions some corrupt officials of the electricity department advised Ashok to draw the power direct from high voltage power transmission lines for his borewell. Ashok never wanted to give up due to odd circumstances and, as a last resort, decided to go as per the advice. But not knowing the repercussion due to lack of knowledge, he naively tried to tap the electric power from the transmission line to run his water pump but sadly lost his life due to electrocution while taking the electric connection leaving behind his wife and son without having any destitution.

Thus Ashok finished his life in absence of a monitoring, counselling, and support system for vulnerable farmers. This narrative brings the story of one out of many such small farmers every year in our country.

The Awakening

Navaratri is a major festival held for nine days every year in the honour of the divine feminine. The two folk dances Garba and Dandiya are played by men and women during these nine days. Garba is a dance form of Gujarat, Rajasthan, and Malwa region of Madhya Pradesh wherein dances are performed around centrally lit statues of the Goddess Durga (Shakti).

This story is set in Mandvi, Kutch in the late 90's. Mandvi is an old, small, and aloof town in the Kutch region of Gujarat and is enclosed in the fort wall. A young and US-educated Jigna Dangar, a resident of Gandhinagar got married to a cloth merchant Ritesh Dangar of Mandvi. The entire region of Kutch did not see a good rainfall since 1990, affecting badly the agricultural activity which has been a way of life for the community in rural areas of

Kutch including Mandvi. After spending some time in Mandvi, Jigna came to know about this calamity of nature. She was told by the people that there has been no rainfall in the village for last more than six years. Jigna met a cross-section of people in Mandvi and was shocked to learn the reason given by the villagers for insufficient rainfall in the area. According to the belief of the Mandvi people, the local clan Goddess was angry with them and had cursed them for allowing their women to perform in the Garba dance during every Navaratri. Since then, to apologise and impress the Goddess, only the men every year during Navaratri had been performing the Garba dance forbidding women to take part in it. Jigna also learned from Mauli Dave, her neighbour about many other restrictions put on the women of the village including their coming out of houses except in the early hours of the morning when they were permitted to go to a distant lake to fetch the water.

Jigna, being highly educated, was stunned to notice that for persistent drought-like conditions in the area, the whole onus was put on women. She made up her mind to change this situation forever and better the lives of the village women. Her husband Ritesh and friend Mauli agreed to support Jigna in this social cause. First of all, they met the officials of the Indian Meteorological Department (IMD) of the Kutch region to know the exact reasons for these geographical conditions. Jigna was told that the intense low-pressure formation over the Tibetan plateau and sometimes the permanent high-pressure cell in the South of the Indian Ocean were the two main reasons behind deficient monsoonal activity over this region. They further advised them to increase the number of trees and vegetation in the area. After knowing the reasons, Jigna and her friend along with an NGO of that area started a tree plantation program and planted more than five thousand plants in Mandvi.

One fine day, when Jigna and Mauli were on their way to the lake along with other village women came across an unconscious person who had fainted due to sunstroke. The ladies helped him to gain consciousness.

He introduced himself as Darsh Sanghvi, a musician from Kutch. At the request of ladies, Darsh played his dhol (drum) and asked them to join him by playing Garba with the drumbeat and the women did so. Since then, Darsh used to play his dhol and the women performed Garba every morning when they used to come to fetch water from the lake. This gave lots of happiness to the women. They asked Darsh to meet village sarpanch, Tejas Nayak to request him for a shelter in the village. They also asked him to try to convince the sarpanch to allow ladies of the village for playing Garba during all the nine days of Navaratra. Sarpanch, being a rational person and impressed by the expertise of Darsh in Gujarati music, allowed the ladies to perform Garba during the ensuing festival. He did not want to continue with the outdated and orthodox customs of the village of prohibiting women to take part in the folk dance. Since then women, along with men, started enjoying the dance in front of the diety every Navaratra.

After eradicating this old age superstition from Mandvi, Jigna and her friends decided to uproot this discriminatory custom from the entire Kutch where ever it existed. To accomplish their endeavour, Jigna took the help of Pranav Bhatt, the president of Andhashraddha Unmoolan Organisation, Pune. Bhatt along with Jigna, Ritesh, Mauli, Darsh, and Tejas carried out intense campaigns in all such areas by playing street plays and Garba dance to eradicate this gender-based inequality in performing the folk dance. Their untiring efforts soon fetched a good result and now Garba is played by men and women both in the entire Kutch region. To add to their happiness, IMD predicted a good rainfall almost after a decade for the entire western country including the Kutch region. Sarpanch Nayak announced to felicitate Jigna and her friends and to organise a Garba competition and rain dance comprising of men and women during the coming Navaratra in the Mandvi region.

The story conveys that droughts, floods, and other natural calamities are natural phenomena. They are not due to the curse of any God/Goddess of a community. People should be ready to face such natural happenings bravely.

Jatra

Diwali is the time for celebrations, enjoyment, and merry-making in the entire country. Kolkata is also no exception. In fact the Diwali – fever starts there right from Shardiya Navaratra when Goddess Durga is worshipped for nine continuous days but this Diwali of the year 1900 had been quite special in Calcutta.

The reasons are three – firstly the Bhoot Chaturdashi celebration (also known as Narak Chaturdashi or the Chhoti Diwali in the northern part of India), the second reason for the celebration is the cultural program titled–"The Jatra". This program is organised and sponsored by the most respected and renowned family of the city, the Thakurs. The enthusiasm for the celebration of the Jatra is increased as it is being celebrated after a decade. It could not be celebrated for the continuous past ten years owing to the demise of female leads immediately after every show in the mysterious circumstances and hence the play remained suspended for so many years by its organising committee. The impact of mystery deaths of the female lead was so high that no actor for the female lead- role used to be willing to perform in the leading lady role. The entire acting fraternity of Kolkata was of the opinion that the play is a haunted one. This time the grandson of Saraswati Devi, the matriarch of the Thakur family. Yash Thakur is back home after acquiring a degree in cinematography from the London School of Performing Arts after four long years. He is accompanied by his girlfriend, a 26 year charming and educated lady, Jacqueline Josh who is born and brought up in a ratiocinative and coherent family from Denmark. So, the Thakur family wanted to celebrate their homecoming in a unique manner and as a part of it they decided to restart the play, "The Jatra". The Thakur family is a joint one comprising of Saraswati Devi (affectionately known as "Baudo Maa") and her two sons – Shambhu Thakur and Bhushan Thakur along with their spouses and kids and a daughter, Rimi.

The organising committee also managed a lady artist to play the role of female lead named Tanushree in the play Jatra. Tanushree also belonged to Bolpur, the hub of theatre artists. Most of the previous female leads of the play were from Bolpur.

Finally, the day of Bhoot Chaturdashi arrived and the people of Kolkata got ready to watch their favourite play Jatra along with their prince charming Yash Thakur and his would-be bride Jacqueline. The play started at it's scheduled time and then it went off so well that the audience was mesmerised and rejoiced it. Yash and Jacqueline also loved the play because of its tight script and memorable dialogues. Everyone returned back to their homes joyfully in a festive mood and the Diwali festival took off well with the commencement of the play. This was going to be a new experience for Jacqueline. However, in the mansion, the late evening became a nightmare for Jacqueline. She started a feeling of some supernatural object around her. She started seeing apparitions in her room. She had a feeling that she was being called by some mysterious voice of a middle-aged woman. First, she felt that this was her hallucinations and she tried to ignore it and decided not to discuss it with anyone including Yash in the mansion. With each passing day, she began to experience such activities on a regular basis. This led her to discuss it with Yash and other family members including Baudo Maa. But to her utter surprise, everyone in the family tried to avert her curiosities and they were trying to discourage Jacqueline from such happenings. At the same time, she also witnessed fear on everybody's face whenever she brought this issue. This made Jacqueline believe that there is something wrong going on in the family and started believing that there are some hidden dark secrets, which the family is trying to hide from her.

Meanwhile, the residents of Kolkata got the shocking news of the mysterious death of Tanushree on the very next day of Bhoot Chaturdashi, the day when the play Jatra was staged. The death of the actor was noticed in the same way as of all the previous lady actors. Jacqueline came to know about this news on TV. Then she closely watched the dress of Tanushree in the retransmission of the news in which she was wearing at the time of her death. It struck her that the middle-aged woman whose apparition she saw in the mansion on the evening of Jatra was also wearing a similar dress. Jacqueline tried to relate the two incidents with the help of Yash by seeing the photographs of earlier female leads of the play Jatra who were found dead after the play. She found strange similarities in their dresses. Jacqueline felt that there was some big secret which the Thakur family was hiding from her and everybody else in the family knew about it except her and Yash.

Jacqueline hatched a plan to know the reasons for this unanswered secret. She took Yash in confidence and without informing the rest of the family, she left for Bolpur, where most of the Jatra female leads including Tanushree came from.

In Bolpur, Yash and Jacqueline found that all the girls who had acted in Jatra were all alumni of a drama school run by Uma Devi who had been running the school for the last three decades. After her demise, the school is managed by her disciple Laboni. To know more about Uma Devi, Yash and Jacqueline approached her old friend Konkana, a renowned yesteryears theatre actor. At Konkana's s place, they saw the photograph of Uma Devi. After looking at it Jacqueline immediately recollected that the photograph is of the lady who used to haunt her in the mansion. Konkana informed that Laboni and a member of the Thakur family were in deep love with each other. Laboni and that member killed Uma Devi to capture the school. They used to kill lady artists from the school to terrorise Saraswati Devi for capturing the mansion which was in the name of Saraswati Devi. The elder son of Saraswati Devi, Shambhu Thakur was involved in anti-social activities including girl trafficking, and was having connections with drug peddlers of Nigeria. Somehow Saraswati Devi came to know about such horrifying activities of her elder son but due to his terror in the family, no one used to speak a single word about it. However, Saraswati Devi who was a brave lady by nature wrote in her will declaring her younger son and her wife the sole owner of her entire property including the mansion. After knowing the misdeeds of Shambhu Thakur through the whispers of villagers and the estranged wife of Shambhu Thakur, Jacqueline immediately went to the police commissioner of Kolkata and got nabbed Shambhu Thakur and Laboni red-handedly and they were sent behind the bar

Since then, Jatra is being staged peacefully and people knew no bounds of their happiness during Bhoot Chaturdashi and subsequent Diwali celebrations. Every year the whole city is decorated with earthen lamps starting from Bhoot Chaturdashi till the Bhai Bheej. Since then the tradition of lighting one earthen lamp on every Bhoot Chaturdashi (Chhoti Diwali) is being followed in the entire country.

The Bond

In a posh society of Andheri, Mumbai, there lived a young couple – Hirendra Narvekar and Priya Kanitkar, along with Hirendra s father, Mr. Dhananjay Narvekar, lovingly called by the couple as – "Baba". Hirendra is a lawyer and Priya, is a college professor. Hirendra's associate, Vilas Mahadik is also his good friend.

On the night of December 31, 2020, New Year's eve, in a fateful incident, Baba fell from their balcony and was admitted to a nearby hospital. ACP Shriniwas Patil, who resembled Baba and was almost of the same age came to the hospital for the investigation. First, he questioned Hirendra in a separate room and then grilled Priya. Hirendra told the ACP about the not-so-congenial relationship of Priya with Baba. Consequently, they had sent their only son Chirag to a boarding school away from this environment of their house. He also informed the ACP that on December 29, the family had been to Matheran to enjoy Christmas and the New Year's festivities but due to heated conversations between Baba and Priya, Priya had left the trip halfway and the family had to return home the very next day of December 30. Then the ACP also took Priya's version of the incidence and then returned.

After completing the investigation, ACP Patil accuses both – Hirendra and Priya of abetment of suicide of Baba and provided evidence of Baba committing suicide. He warned them not to leave the hospital's premises till he looked at other angles of the ongoing investigation. The very next day, ACP visited the hospital and informed Hirendra in absence of Priya that most likely Priya had attempted to kill Baba by pushing him from the terrace on the night of December 31 and later arrested Priya and puts her into police custody. Hirendra requested ACP Patil and asked him to drop – the "attempt to murder" charges against Priya. ACP told Hirendra that the only way to save his wife was that to confess the crime and took Priya's charges to his head. Hirendra did so and both were put under police custody – Hirendra for the attempt to murder and Priya for being a witness. After passing a few more days, the hospital informed them that Baba had regained consciousness and requested the hospital authorities to call Hirendra, Priya, and ACP Patil. On their arrival, Baba narrated the whole incidence and confessed that his falling from the terrace was a mere accident. Later ACP Patil admitted that he and Baba had planned to teach the couple a lesson about their misbehavior towards Baba by converting the accident into an attempt to murder incidence. The couple realized their mistake and pledged in front of ACP Patil and Baba not to repeat such disrespectful behavior towards any elder and apologized to Baba for his mental agony over the years. ACP Patil also thanked Baba and regretted to Hirendra and Priya for putting them under stress for the last few days. He told them that he and Baba did so to remind Hirendra and Priya that a family is made of aging parents also and that this bonding between the family members is a must for a happy life. Since then the couple lived happily with Baba. They also did not forget to thank ACP Patil to make them understand the real joy of family bonding.

The Relationship

Amit Deshmukh and Girija Shinde were schoolmates in a public school in Colaba, Mumbai during the year 2010. When they grew up Girija took up the job of an executive in an ad agency in Colaba while Amit topped the MBA course at Mumbai University and was looking for a lucrative job of his taste. He left no stone unturned in getting a job of his choice but could not succeed. This led to his gradual frustration. Ultimately he took up the job of marketing executive in a sports management company situated in Bandra.

However, he was not satisfied with the job and kept on looking for a better one but in vain. This made him irritative by nature and he started feeling that nowadays employers prefer ladies to males having the same qualifications for any white-collar jobs.

Amit and Girija have been dating for the last three years and we're in a good relationship. In the meantime, Girija got an important assignment for one year from her office and was being sent to Bengaluru for the same. She discussed this project with Amit and told him that while in Bengaluru she might not be able to connect with Amit frequently owing to the hectic nature of the project. After knowing this Amit got possessive of Girija and asked her not to take up this project so that they could be in regular touch with each other. He did not believe in keeping a long-distance relationship for such a big period. Although Girija denied going for the project at Amit's request but being a career-minded lady, repentance grew up in her. A few days later Amit wanted to take Girija out to a party, thrown by his colleagues at a sports management company to celebrate the promotion of their CEO, Mr. Shantanu.

However, due to some prior official commitments the same evening, Girija could not accept it and despite Amit's repeated requests showed her reluctance. Amit took the refusal to his heart and started seeing it as a fallout of Girija's inability to go to Bengaluru owing to his request. Her refusal made him so upset that he told Girija that he would be not meeting her anymore and rushed away from there. There was no communication between them for the last two and a half months.

On the other hand, Amit's parents, Mr. Narayanrao Deshmukh and Mrs. Premlata Deshmukh were unaware of this new development. They knew that the two youngsters are in a relationship for a significant number of times and now they wanted to get them engaged soon. They discussed it with Amit who informed them that they were no more in a relationship for the last couple of months. They wanted to know from Amit, the reasons for the break – up but on every such occasion Amit did not open up. Amit's father decided to find out the reason since he and his wife felt that Amit and Girija would make a nice couple. So Narayanrao first spoke to Amit and Girija's common friends as well as from some of their office colleagues. Finally, their common friend, Suman Arora, informed Narayanrao that Amit has been feeling insecure and jealous of Girija over Girija's career growth and was passing through a phase of internal conflict. Amit's dialectics forced him to take such an extreme decision. Girija was also in a melancholy mood due to Amit's adamancy over her project assignment. Suman added that their love relationship was converted into an estranged one due to the above reasons. She concluded that Amit's CEO's party incidence in which Girija did not want to go proved to be the catalyst and almost ended their relationship. After getting to know the reasons for his son Amit's break-up with Girija, Narayanrao tried to counsel his son and asked him to give a second thought to his decision. However, Amit justified the break-up and told his father that Girija's behavior towards him had changed ever since she got the Bengaluru project. He also told him that Girija should prioritize him over her job.

After hearing Amit's reply, Narayanrao wanted to know Girija's side of the story. To do so he planned a lunch at a nearby hotel and asked Amit and his wife Premlata to accompany him for it. Without informing them he also invited Girija for the lunch who promptly accepted it due to her respect towards Narayanrao and his wife. In the hotel, Amit and his mother were surprised to see Girija accompanying Narayanrao. Narayanrao then informed them that Girija had come at his invitation. During lunch, Narayanrao made Amit and Girija sit face to face with each other and made everybody at ease by cutting jokes about his younger days. In this relaxed environment, Amit and Girija came to talking terms and opened up with each other. After the pre-lunch drinks, Girija asked Amit's parents if she wanted to talk to Amit about some issues in private. Appreciating this, Amit's parents moved towards the recreation room of the hotel to leave the two together. Girija expressed her unhappiness about Amit's telling his parents only one side of the story of their break-up. She further asked Amit why he was not serious about his career and stopped applying for jobs matching his qualifications. She also questioned his possessiveness about her going to Bengaluru to better her job prospects. Amit had no answers to her questions and he kept mum which further annoyed Girija and she left the hotel after paying respects to Amit's parents. She also ranged up Narayanrao for her inappropriate behavior at the hotel.

When Deshmukhs were heading back to their home from the hotel, Amit recollected his last fight with Girija which took before their break-up. Girija had been confronting him for not showing up at the job interviews and for his casual approach to his career. She had yelled at Amit due to his such a lethargic approach in his life he had lost an opportunity of getting a job in Boston, USA. All this had made Amit upset and he had asked her to leave her house.

Twenty days had passed since they visited the hotel and Deshmukhs were having their 35th marriage anniversary the next day. Amit listened to his father inviting Girija to the function. Amit then asked his father why he had been always remembering Girija and taking her side. Amit's father then explained to him that he had felt Amit's s internal tussle going on for some time because he dislikes the present job, not getting a job of his choice, and Girija's vertical growth of her career. He added that he had found Girija an intelligent, practical, and composed girl over some time and she had been trying to persuade Amit to work harder and take life seriously to achieve the success he deserved. However, instead of understanding her motives, Amit had not been taking her advice seriously and ultimately broke his three-year relationship with her.

After hearing his father and with introspection regarding his relationship with Girija Amit realized his improper behavior towards her, he went to Girija's house and apologized to her for all his ill-treatment over the past three months. Girija felt happy that now Amit has realized his shortcomings and was ready to take on life seriously. They together came back to Amit's house to celebrate the marriage anniversary of Amit's parents. Seeing them together, the happiest person was Amit's father. He told them that they have given him the best gift on his 35th marriage anniversary. The celebration went off till late at night and became a memorable one for Deshmukh. In the function itself, Amit and Girija pledged not to allow any misunderstandings to creep into their relationship. They also announced to take their relationship to a next level when Amit proposed to Girija for marriage, which Girija happily accepted. With this announcement, the euphoria of Amit's parents knew no bounds.

London Calling

In Gandhinagar, Gujarat there lived two fast friends, Suresh Patel and Prabhat Desai, who were in the export business of clothes and readymades. People in Gandhinagar used to give examples of their friendship. Both of them had an intense desire of visiting London. However, money was an issue for both of them. Prabhat was lucky in arranging the money by selling a part of his ancestral property. But, Suresh did not have any such source. Prabhat flew to London after completing all the formalities and asked Suresh to join him in London after arranging the funds and then the two would enjoy the trip.

Despite many attempts including approaching the banks, Suresh remained unsuccessful and dropped the idea of going to London with a heavy heart. At the same time, he felt betrayed and started resenting his friend Prabhat. Prabhat with the help of a few other Gujarati cloth merchants settled in London also expanded his business while in London and soon became a business tycoon in the Eastern and Northern parts of London.

After spending almost 5 years in London he came back to India and was now an affluent trader. He wanted to invest in his home state Gujarat. He aimed to contribute a little to the development of his home state so that he could give back to his homeland whatever he had earned from his overseas trip. On the other hand, Suresh was busy in his business activities along with his two sons, Pratik and Dileep. The elder one Pratik wanted to expand and grow his father's s business with his hard work while the younger one, Dileep was a rapturous person, whimsical by nature. He used to have fun rashly driving his bike on the roads of Gandhinagar and was a speed enjoyer. Since bad habits die hard, he was booked by police in a hit-and-run case on an occasion.

After knowing that his father could not fulfill his dream of visiting London for want of money, he wanted to take his father on a London trip by hook or by crook. He applied for a UK visa for himself and his father. Although the visa application of his father got through, his visa application was turned down by the British embassy due to his involvement in the hit and run case which the case was still on in the lower court. This was shocking for him and put him in a melancholy mood.

On one fine day, Dileep's childhood friend, Amar Upadhyay introduced Dileep to his roommate Avinash Mehta. Amar informed Dileep that Avinash would soon be going to the UK. Learning the intense desire of Dileep of visiting London, Avinash introduced him to his travel agent, Velajibhai Garodia. Garodia assured Dileep that he would make sure of arranging a passport and UK – visa for him but for his services he would charge Rs. 10 lakhs from him. Pratik, Dileep's elder brother was also willing to send Dileep and his father to the UK to fulfill their dreams. To arrange the money demanded by Garodia, Pratik borrowed money from dubious money – lenders of Gandhinagar. Dileep and

Pratik were unaware that Garodia and his associates were part of an international racket. Although the racket was busted many times by the police, it was still running smoothly with the help of some corrupt politicians and bureaucrats of Gandhinagar.

Garodia and his friends used to trap those who were desperate to go overseas but were unable to do so because of their involvement in anti-social activities. Now, Dileep was also in their trap. After receiving hefty money from Dileep's brother, Garodia arranged a fake passport and visa UK for Dileep and also booked two tickets for London in the names of Dileep and his father Suresh. When he handed over the documents to Dileep, his joy knew no bounds. He was delighted to inform his father that the two would be flying to London on coming Monday without telling his father how Garodia had arranged the documents for him. Everyone in Suresh's family was overjoyed.

After all, it was not only Suresh's longtime dream that was getting fulfilled but also they could tell Prabhat that they were also capable of visiting London. On the D – day, the father and son duo reached the airport much in advance to board the flight. The family members also joined to see them off. After reaching London the next morning, the first thing that Suresh did was to give a message to Prabhat which read – "Hey Prabhat, I am in London". Back home in India, Pratik started getting phone calls from the money-lender to return his money soon. Pratik assured him of the same and started exploring the options of arranging the money. But, despite his best efforts and running from pillar to post he was falling short of borrowed money. The moneylender warned Pratik of dire consequences if he could not return his money in a week. However, Pratik became helpless.

On this, the moneylender showed his real color and phoned the Indian embassy in London to that an Indian named, Dileep, had entered London on fake documents. On receiving the tip-off, the London police came into action and soon arrested Dileep for traveling to London on fake documents. After hearing the case, the local

London – court awarded three years of rigorous imprisonment to Dileep. Hearing this, his father got unconscious and was later admitted to a hospital. After getting discharged from the hospital, his father applied to the Indian embassy in London requesting them to see that his stay in London was extended till his son completed the jail term.

The same was agreed upon by the London authorities and Suresh started doing the job of a salesman in a London outlet. On the day of the acquittal of Dileep, the Indian Embassy came into action and sent them back to India with a detailed report on them. On landing at the Gandhinagar airport another problem was waiting for them. Indian police arrested Dileep on the charges of traveling to

London on forged documents and defaming the Indian government and putting him under its custody. Later, Gandhinagar's court sentenced him to three years imprisonment. On the complaint of Suresh, police also busted the ongoing racket run by Garodia and his associates for arranging forged passports and visa to any country and all were put underbar.

It is good to be passionate about one's dream but to fulfill the dream through illegal means lands not only the individual in trouble but also defames the country. When Yashodhara, the wife of Prabhat heard that the family of Suresh was undergoing mountains of sorrow breaking, she reminded Prabhat of their long-time friendship and insisted that Prabhat should bail them out from their deep sorrowful time. The two then decided to offer Suresh, his wife Malini, and his son Pratik a trip to London. Hearing this, the family was overwhelmed by its generosity of Prabhat. After a couple of days, they left for London for a week. In the flight, Suresh whispered in the ears of his wife, Malini, and said – "London was calling them".

The Accident

Indrajeet Naik, a driver in Mumbai, was a pretentious man and had lots of dreams in his eyes. He wanted to have his own travel – agency. One day he met a person named Dhanraj Patil and when Patil came to know about the ambitions of Indrajeet, he offered him to join his fleet of taxis as a driver during day times and to help him in his hooch business during the night. Although Indrajeet was a hard-working and honest person to make quick money to fulfill his dreams, he readily accepted the offer. So, he started playing taxi during day time and at night, he used to deliver the illegal liquor to the addresses provided by Patil. After a few weeks of doing the dual jobs of Patil, Indrajeet's s conscious did not allow him to carry on.

He, therefore, left the job in Patil and joined a Mumbai industrialist, Mr. Rajyavardhan

Chauhan as his driver. Chauhan had only one son named Shankar Chauhan, who was in the film-making business. Indrajeet used to pick – up and drop Shankar at the Film City. With his punctuality, discipline, and hard work Indrajeet soon became a blue-eyed man of Chauhan's family. Florina Coutinho, a girl from Paris befriended Shankar on a social media site a few months ago and at Shankar's request came to Mumbai to meet him. Observing Florina's difficulty in English conversation, Shankar asked Indrajeet's sister Jaya Naik to start teaching spoken English to Florina. Shankar also asked Indrajeet to take Florina in and around Mumbai City to show her the places of a visitor's delight. Gradually over the days while traveling Flourina got impressed with Indrajeet's desire of owning a travel agency. She further suggested he to think of beginning a start-up by raising funds using the government's scheme. When days passed Florina and Indrajeet started liking each other and ultimately fell in love. Slowly Indrajeet also came to know about the bitter relationship between Shankar and his father and also Shankar's problem in his business with his overseas business partner Mr. David Johnson. On the other hand, Shankar smelt the growing closeness of Florina and Indrajeet.

Annoyed by Indrajeet over this issue, Shankar changed his mind to continue as his guarantor for securing the bank's loan taken by Indrajeet to start his travel agency. To show Florina Mumbai's traditions, Indrajeet and Florina planned to visit a nearby Garba night. The same evening Shankar asked Florina to accompany him to the premiere show of a newly released Bollywood film. However, Florina was reluctant to go to the movie as her understanding of Hindi was weak. But on Shankar's repeated requests she became ready to go. On the way, Florina confessed to Shankar that she had developed emotions for Indrajeet and wanted to marry him. Hearing this, Shankar got astonished.

Driving his car in a fit of rage, Shankar eventually met with an accident at a checkpoint killing two police constables on the spot and making an elderly person badly injured. Florina was shocked to witness the horrifying car accident and asked Shankar to take the three for medical help immediately. However, Shankar snubbed Florina and said that if he got down to do the same, the on-lookers gathered at the accident site would hand over him to the police. Therefore he drove away from the car at its fullest speed and managed to escape from the accident site. Florina got horrified over this act of Shankar. On the other hand, Indrajeet started roaming around the streets of Mumbai in a melancholy mood. Coincidentally Indrajeet came near the same accident site and anxiously wanted to know about the accident after parking his car at a nearby place. When he came to know about the severity of the crime he immediately left the site. A few hours later a team of crime police reached the spot and started their investigation. The footage of the CCTV camera at the accident spot showed Indrajeet's car parked near the site. After finding that the car belonged to Mr. Chauhan, the police team reached Chauhan's house and got to know that it's the driver is Indrajeet, who worked for Chauhan.

Indrajeet was summoned to the police station for further inquiry. The police also came to know that in the past Indrajeet was involved in hooch distribution in the city. They immediately put Indrajeet under police custody for committing the serious crime although Indrajeet claimed his ignorance about the event as he had arrived late at the accident site. Police continued their investigation and interviewed several eye-witnesses of the crime and came to know that after the accident they had seen a car fleeing away in which the son Shankar of industrialist Chauhan was in the driver's seat accompanied by a foreign lady. Eyewitnesses also told police the timing of the accident and running away from the car driven by Shankar. Based on statements of the eyewitnesses and a few other important pieces of evidence the police team reached Chauhan's place and questioned Shankar about his passing away from the accident site and about a foreign lady sitting beside him. When Shankar's father came to know that the police team was on its way to catch his son in the hit and run case he used his influence to pressurize the police team not to implicate his son and frame Indrajeet for the crime who was already in police custody. Since the investigative team was aware of the powerfulness of Chauhan's family in the city it agreed to drop Shankar's name from the charge sheet. However, the police team was on the lookout for a foreign lady who, according to the eyewitnesses, was sitting beside Shankar in the car which was seen running away from the accident spot at the time of the accident. On the other hand, as a precaution, the father-son duo asked Florina not to come out of their house till the matter was settled. Police put up the case in the criminal court for a hearing. The son Anmol Katkar of the elderly person who got badly injured and had been practicing in the same court appeared for Indrajeet. Indrajeet briefed Anmol on the entire episode of the accident. Indrajeet also informed Chinmay that Shankar was driving the car with his friend Florina sitting beside him and the two had passed through the accident site.

Meanwhile, Florina text-messaged Indrajeet that she was made to hide in Chauhan's house because she was the eye–witness to the accident done by Shankar. But seeing the brutality of crime and apathy of Shankar towards the deceased constables she wanted to narrate the entire incident in the court as a witness. Indrajeet discussed the message of Florina with Anmol who produced the text – message in the court the very next day. Consequently, the court ordered the police to rescue Florina from Chauhan's house and present her in court. After completely hearing the lawyers of the two sides the judge found Shankar guilty and sentenced him to life imprisonment. Two-year imprisonment to his father for forcing Florina to hide in his house was also awarded. Indrajeet thanked Chinmay for all the support and for making him free from a false case. He also thanked Florina for her courage to speak out the truth in the court and get the real culprit booked. To this, Florina replied that although Shankar was his long-time friend through a dating app, and she was a guest of Shankar, her conscious did not allow her to continue such a friendship. Had she known the cruel character of Shankar she would not have befriended him. She also added that one should be careful while making friends on apps and not make advances in such friendships without necessary checks. Six months had passed since then and Indrajeet and Florina were now a happily married couple.

The Land

Farmers in Siliguri, a district of Darjeeling situated in the north of West Bengal have been facing a serious problem of selling their lands forcibly to a lobby of powerful and super-rich money-lenders and then were compelled to work as farm laborers in their lands. This story revolves around the similar plight of Arindam Bagchi whose father Somdev Bagchi was forced to sell his land and was employed as a watchman on his land. One day when Arindam visited his father at his workplace, he saw the cunning landlord Uday Mukherjee mercilessly beating his father for being late for work. Arindam felt it to his heart and challenged Mukherjee that he would not only get back his land from him but also would bring him to the task. The arrogant Mukherjee drove away both – the father and the son from there and warned them not to roam around near the land. The family of Arindam was so frightened by the warning of Mukherjee that they shifted to Jhargram from Siliguri. Arindam and his father started working as porters in the vegetable market for their livelihood. The market was controlled by some local goons who used to extort money from the shopkeepers.

One day when Arindam saw the goons compelling an old man for extortion, Arindam could not stop himself and beat up the goons with the help of some shopkeepers and ultimately landed in the local jail. In the jail, he met Gautam Adhikari as his inmate. Adhikari was a powerful gangster who had the patronage of a local MLA, Shubhankar Deb. After coming out of jail Arindam joined hands with Adhikari and soon earned his name in the crime world of Jhargram. At the behest of Adhikari Arindam murdered the popular mayor of the city, Tapan Das. Tapan and Adhikari were professional rivals. In a week, Adhikari bailed Arindam out by fabricating the murder as suicide with the help of false testimonials from the people present there.

Soon Arindam became a much sought-after member of Adhikari's gang. Adhikari sent Arindam to a neighboring country for getting trained in looting, extortions, and land-grabbing. When Arindam returned after the training he was in a new avatar of a hardcore criminal. Now Arindam's priority was to settle down the issues of the vegetable vendors of the market where he and his father used to work as porters. To give immediate relief to the vegetable vendors, he announced in the market that he would arrange to send their produce to the wholesale market so that they would get a better price. Soon Arindam became a prominent member of Adhikari's gang. One day Ajay and Sanjay, the two members of Adhikari's gang informed Adhikari that they could not annex the land owned by a prominent businessman, Pandora of Siliguri. Since Arindam now had a hatred for Siliguri, he promptly offered Adhikari to give this task to him. Arindam went to Siliguri, shot Pandole to death in front of his family, and got their land registered in his name.

Although Arindam was arrested for this act, Adhikari again bailed him out. With his influence, Adhikari put the onus for this murder on Pandora's uncle. Now next target of Arindam was Adhikari himself as he wanted to take over his gang himself. By now Arindam had become a blue-eyed man of Adhikari. He invited Arindam to his birthday party. He utilized this occasion and murdered Adhikari and manipulated the incident and framed the charges of murder of Adhikari on Ajay and Sanjay, the two members of Adhikari's gang. Arindam was now the gangster of the town and was known in Jhargram as Arindam Da.

He used to help and back all those people who were needy. On one occasion a teenage boy, Nishant had come from Siliguri on foot to meet Arindam for a livelihood as Nishant had become an orphan, due to the demise of both of his parents during the Corona pandemic. Knowing that Nishant belonged to his native place, Siliguri, and was in deep trouble, Arindam treated him as his younger brother and assured him that he would not only arrange a job for him but he would also fund his education. Despite his good work towards the downtrodden people of his area, his own family and would-be bride Kanchan disowned him due to his anti-lawful activities. Dejected by his people, Arindam became all alone, and to revenge the society for his present-day conditions, he started expanding his gang and became a more dreaded gangster. Extortions, land-grabbings, and kidnappings for a ransom became his lifestyle.

Arindam now wanted to focus on Siliguri, his hometown, and zeroed upon his father's land which was forcibly grabbed by the cunning landlord Uday Mukherjee. Arindam killed Uday after taking his father's land back from him. He was happy that he fulfilled his pledge taken a few years back. An elated Arindam shared this news with his father Somdev but Somdev refused to own his piece of land due to the cohesive method used by his son in getting back the land. This was a jolt to Arindam as he wanted to reunite his family and get away from the world of crime. He assured his father that he would mend his ways and soon join politics. However, his father refused to live with Arindam. His fiancee Kanchan also expressed her unhappiness over the unlawful activities of Arindam and informed him that her marriage was settled with a software techie and would leave Siliguri forever to settle permanently in Kolkata.

All these developments aggravated Arindam and disappointed with the circumstances he left Siliguri in a fit of rage. He – started and re-joined his activities as a gangster. One of the MLAs of Jhargram, Avinash Chaudhary came to know that Arindam was back and was also interested in contesting the upcoming assembly elections from his constituency on a rival political party's ticket. He knew that Arindam was very popular amongst the poor and downtrodden people of the area due to his soft corner for this section of electorates. This made Chaudhary worried about his votes getting divided. He thought of a deadly plan to get rid of Arindam forever. To execute his plan he lured the two brothers Ajay and Sanjay to shrug off Arindam by killing him to grab the opportunity of their taking over the place of Arindam in his gang. Avinash also assured the duo that he would take care of the legal aspect after post-the murder of Arindam. Foreseeing a golden opportunity coming their way to rule the crime world of Jhargram and the neighboring areas, the two brothers promptly accepted the offer. As per the plan, Ajay and Sanjay attacked Arindam's house on a mission to kill him. After many rounds of firing between Ajay and Sanjay and their henchmen and Arindam, Arindam managed to escape and ran away from his house. After running for about half an hour Arindam reached the vegetable market, where he and his father Somdev worked. Arindam phoned Nishant to ask his gang – members to reach the vegetable market to counter the henchmen of Ajay and Sanjay who had been chasing him right from his house. Instead of alerting Arindam's gang – members, Nishant proceeded alone towards the vegetable – market with a loaded pistol.

When Arindam's father saw Arindam hiding in the market, he informed the police about the possible gang– war in the market. On its arrival, the police arrested Ajay and

Sanjay and his henchmen to save the area from a possible shootout. Arindam finally surrendered himself to the police. In the meantime, Nishant reached the vegetable market and fired five rounds at Arindam in a nick of time. Arindam got a shock of his life and asked Nishant why he fired at him. To this, Nishant replied that he was the grandson of the businessman, Pandora whom Arindam had killed and since then he wanted to take revenge on Arindam. Arindam was rushed to a nearby hospital but he succumbed to the bullet injuries. As soon as the news of the death of Arindam reached the vegetable – market, a shock wave was created and all the vendors were seen in tears, except his father Somdev. Somdev told the S. I. Devang Patil that it was a society that converted a gentle and disciplined boy Arindam into a hardcore criminal. His father started laughing and told S. I. Patil that although his son has amassed many acres of land through criminal activities he will require only a few meters of land for his last rites. Meanwhile, through intelligence reports, the CP of Jhargram came to know that the MLA Avinash Chaudhary was promoting goons and vagabonds of the area to win the assembly elections. It also came to the notice of CP that Avinash had hatched a plan to kill Arindam through Ajay and Sanjay. To stop lawlessness in the region and the growing influence of Chaudhary in the crime world of the area, Devang Patil, S. I. followed the orders of his bosses and killed MLA Chaudhary in a fake encounter and briefed the media that Chaudhary was caught red-handed after he was seen of negotiating smuggled illegal weapons to terrorize the voters of his constituency.

The Friendship

Time - Period, The year, 2021.

Main Characters - Chitaranjan Thakkar (Cheeku), Prateek Patel (Preet), Haribhai - the Godman, Darshan Bhai (Chitaranjan's father), Hassan Miyan - the painter, Kavin Meriwala, Cheeku and Preet' s common friend, Kanjilal Desai, the local art - dealer, Kinjal Suwalka, Preet's girlfriend, and, Abhinav Gupta (Abhi), the method actor.

Protagonists - Chitaranjan Thakkar (Cheeku), Prateek Patel (Preet), Darshan Bhai (Chitaranjan's father), and Kinjal Suwalka (Preet's girlfriend).

Antagonists - Haribhai - the Godman, and Kanjilal Desai, the local art - dealer.

Supporting Roles-Hassan Miyan-the painter, Kavin Meriwala, Cheeku and Preet's common friend, and Abhinav Gupta (Abhi), the method actor.

THE PLOT

In the final quarter of the year 2021, somewhere in Silvassa, in the Union Territory of Dadra Nagar Haveli and Daman and Diu, two childhood friends, Chitaranjan Thakkar (Cheeku) and Prateek Patel (Preet) aspire to invest in a real estate project called-"The Second End", located near the scenic Fatehpura area and their residence of Silvassa. They currently work as pharmaceutical sales representatives, while hoping to make quick money through a cunning Godman, Haribhai, who promises to triple their profit. The Godman turns out to be a part of a larger con, and his scheme is discovered by the police. As a result, Cheeku and Preet are scammed out of Rs. 2,00,000 (or 2,00,000 rupees).

Cheeku ' s father, Darshan Bhai, runs a small local tea stall, in which hangs a painting from a prominent artiste, named, Hassan Miyan (based on the late extremely famous painter, M. F. Hussain). The piece was gifted to Darshan Bhai as a sign of their close friendship by Hassan Miyan, before his rise to prominence and eventual death. Upon learning that Darshan Bhai's tea - stall painting is highly coveted, Preet comes up with another idea to secure an investment with "The Second End", - secretly replace the painting with an identical fake one, and then loan the original for cash. Initially hesistent, but desperate, Cheeku assists in the plan, along with their common friend, Kavin Meriwala, an avid painter, who begrudgingly agrees to compose an exact copy of the piece himself.

With the switch successful, Cheeku and Preet mortgage the original painting to a local art - dealer, Kanjilal Desai. Shortly thereafter, however, Desai informs Cheeku that the painting he received is a fake one and that someone else had tried to sell the same painting to another dealer. Desai convinces Cheeku, that either, Preet had double - crossed him, or that his father had been lying about the painting's authenticity. Cheeku returns the money back to Desai, and, angrilly confronts Preet, who indeed went to a separate dealer, but was sent by Kavin for an art surveu only. Cheeku then meets his father, and accuses him of confabulating a friendship. Angered by the accusations and hurt by Cheeku's loss of the painting, Darshan Bhai kicks him out of the house.

The Hassan Miyan painting, however, was an original all along, and Desai - whom Hassan Miyan hated and never lent his work to - had cheated Cheeku and Preet out of the painting. Desai then publically humiliates Darshan Bhai by telling the press, that Darshan Bhai never had a friendship with Hassan Miyan, and that the stories of Hassan Miyan making his paintings at Darshan Bhai's tea - stall are all false.

Hoping to redeem themselves, Cheeku and Preet devise a plan to take advantage of Desai's own greed in order to get the painting back for Darshan Bhai. For the help for this purpose, they included Kavin and Kinjal

Suwalka (Preet's girlfriend) in the plan. They hired a method actor, Abhinav Gupta (Abhi) to pose as - "Umesh Shukla", a fictitious international NRI artiste from Ahmedabad, Gujarat, whose work has yet to be exhibited in India. The group successfully lures Desai into funding a fabricated NGO and conducting Shukla's supposed lucrative first exhibition in India, in exchange for the tea - stall painting.

Abhinav and Kavin narrowly retrieve the painting on the day of the held exhibition, just before Desai realizes that Abhinav is a fraud. He confronts the place and owners of the fake NGO (all Abhinav's men), but encounters Cheeku, Preet, and Darshan Bhai. Cheeku and Preet demands that Desai should publically retract his earlier statements about Darshan Bhai, or else be arrested for selling fake paintings and creating the fictitious - "Umesh Shukla" himself (since Desai was tricked earlier into funding the fake NGO). Realising his defeat, Desai tries to offer money, but Darshan Bhai declines and chastises Desai, for his greed being the reason, Hassan Miyan never worked with large art curators like him (Desai).

Desai holds a televised news - conference the next morning, apologizing for his previous accusations against Darshan Bhai. Hassan Miyan's piece is returned to Darshan Bhai's shop, after the father - son duo fully reconcile. Kavin, whose own paintings were used as Abhinav's works from the earlier times in Ahmedabad, where the so - called - "Umesh Shukla" (Abhinav Gupta was based), is offered his own local art - exhibition, attended by a much happier lot of Cheeku, Preet, Darshan Bhai, and Kinjal.

Two Sitsters

Setting - New Bhuj, Gujarat.

Time - Period - The year, 2021.

Main Characters-Renuka, Anuja, Uncle Vinayak Desai, Renuka and Anuja's father, Mr. Manohar Bhatt, Renuka and Anuja's mother, Mrs. Somabai Bhatt, Urmila Desai, Uncle Desai's wife, Mohan Patel, and Narayan Joshi.

Protagonists - Narayan, Mohan, Renuka, and Anuja.

Antagonists - Uncle Desai, and his wife, Urmila Desai.

Supporting Role - Renuka and Anuja's father and mother.

THE PLOT

In New Bhuj, the elder of the two sisters, Renuka, is getting married, and there is festivity in the household. Elders in the village advise her to visit a temple before groom arrives, and so is accompanied by her younger sister, Anuja, and their cunning Uncle, Mr. Vinayak Desai, and his wife, Urmila. While on their way back, Uncle Desai notices in the newspaper that the groom's family had met with a fatal accident, while coming to the village. Renuka and Anuja's father, Mr. Manohar Bhatt is paralysed after the shocking news. The villagers shun Renuka as an ill omen. Soon, the family starts facing financial troubles, so they attempt to till their piece of infertile land to get some money. When nothing works out, Renuka and Anuja's mother, Mrs. Somabai Bhatt, requests Uncle Vinayak Desai to take Renuka to Ahmedabad for a job. Initially, hesitant, Uncle Desai agrees to the persuasion, but requests the mother not to ask any further questions about Renuka's whereabouts in the future.

Uncle Desai puts Renuka into prostitution, and she starts sending money to her family every month. Things get better for the family, and, Uncle Desai finds a groom for Anuja, a young idealist, Mohan Patel, who works with an NGO. Renuka visits New Bhuj for Anuja's marriage, but their mother, Mrs. Somabai Bhatt does not allow her to take part in any marriage - related activities, because of Renuka's unfortunate marriage incident, and, after getting to know, in which profession, Renuka works in Ahmedabad. When Anuja gets to know about this, she questions their mother, and convinces her to accept Renuka. When Renuka decides to leave marriage and village, Mohan's activist friend, Narayan Joshi proposes Renuka for marriage, in spite of knowing her past. Renuka stays back in the village, with an aim of never to return to her life as a prostitute in Ahmedabad, where as, Mohan and Anuja successfully complete their marriage ceremony.

The Love

Somewhere in the midst of the Mumbai City, in the months of March - May 2022, lives Radio Jockey (R. J.) Amrita Kamble, who works in an FM Radio - Big FM. She is loved by the entire Mumbai City because of her energetic voice and good attitude. She is against the thoughts of being in love and relationships initially, and tells her boss, Mr. Samrat Patel that she would never fall in love. In the month of March 2022, R. J. Amrita was awarded the youngest R. J. achiever award for the year - 2021, at the age of 23 years because of her contribution and her dedicated work towards her FM Radio - Big FM. The award ceremony, which was a glittery affair, was attended by the big - wigs of the radio, TV, and the film industry, or in short, the entertainment industry.

Amongst the attendees of the award ceremony was Milind Pathak, a rich business man, who also invested in the organisation of the music concerts in the Mumbai City, because of his love towards the Indian Bollywood music. Milind had one day observed Amrita, some two - three months back, when Amrita was helping the traffic police clear the traffic, while Milind was on his way to his office in Bandra. In the award - ceremony, Milind saw Amrita taking the award and recognised her. After the award ceremony got over, Milind met Amrita and befriended her. Gradually, they became best friends, and Milind fell in love with Amrita, and genuinely wanted to see her happy always.

Their friendship slowly became the talk of the town, and became a regular affair in entertainment magzines, as a love story, and due to which, her boss, Samrat Patel teased Amrita because of that, and laughed off her earlier vow, which she had made to him, that she would never fall in love in her life.

Once, R. J. Amrita, while hosting her show, in the month of February 2022 had got a call from one Swati Nagpure, a BPO employee from Andheri, who asked her what to answer to her boyfriend, as her boyfriend, Dileep Shetty, a web designer from Borivalli was going to propose her on the Valentine's Day. Dileep, who was already rejected 24 times by different girls, yet was optimistic about someone agreeing on him. Amrita asked Swati to listen to her heart and break - up with Dileep, if she is not happy with him, or does not see any future with him.

Convinced with the advice, Amrita gave her, Swati rejected Dileep's proposal and broke up with him. This disheartened Dileep to a great extent. After getting rejected by Swati, Dileep is dejected and is in a very bad mood, but is somehow consoled by his father, Mr. Ramakant Shetty. Later on, after eight months, when Dileep learns that it was because of Amrita's advice, which she gave to Swati during her programme, had Swati rejected him, he decided to take revenge on Amrita by following her to the Silvassa trip, which Amrita had planned along with her friends to spend her Diwali vacations. Dileep came to know about Amrita's this trip along with her friends through her Facebook page and decides to follow her on this trip. For the purpose of taking Amrita's photographs on her trip, Dileep also takes along with him, his photographer friend, and a colleague from his office, Malhar Kamat. After secretly following Amrita on her trip, along with his friend, Malhar, he, with the help of Malhar takes her photos and after allegedly morphing them by showing Amrita with himself, he posts them on various websites, with the photographs showing Amrita having a romantic affair with him. Dileep does so in order to ruin Amrita's reputation.

Dileep and Malhar, the photographer, manages to get information about Amrita's Silvassa trip along with her friends, through her Facebook page and boards the same bus, which she had boarded. Dileep manages to initiate his talks with Amrita and befriends her. However, at a later stage during this trip, Dileep falls in love with Amrita, as he starts spending time with her in the trip. Although, Dileep starts loving Amrita, but he is not able to overcome the pain of being dumped by

Swati, on Amrita's advise, and with the help of Malhar, he posts the photographs taken by Malhar on the websites. However, on the next day, he deletes these photographs from the websites.

Amrita also secretly starts feeling for Dileep, and deep in her heart, also knows that Dileep is also feeling for her, during their stay in Silvassa. However, some days after the trip, once when she is invited by Dileep for his birthday party at his home, in the month of December 2022, she goes to Dileep's room and finds her morphed photographs of her Silvassa trip with Dileep in his laptop and understands that for what purpose, Dileep had saved these photographs in his laptop and what he wanted to do with them. This makes her angry and hurts her a lot. Amrita comes to the conclusion that Dileep does not love her, but was just using her name to become famous.

When Amrita angrily left the party, Dileep tried to stop her and revealed about his anger on Amrita, when he came to know that her advise forced Swati to reject him, after being questioned by Amrita about the photographs. Amrita realised that Dileep had planned a revenge on her, and this hurted her even more. She told Dileep not to talk with her henceforth, and decided to do a break - up with Dileep, and move on in life.

After some days, Milind comes to know about Dileep and Amrita's Silvassa trip, calls Dileep to his office and warns him to stay away from Amrita and avoid hurting her. A few days later, Milind proposes Amrita for marriage, to which, Amrita chooses not to respond to. Then, on one fine day, Dileep calls her on her programme - Radio Love Line, which she used to host on the Big FM Radio, and reminds her that without her, his life has become monotonous, and he misses her a lot.

Amrita decides to ignore Dileep's calls and messages, and instead, agrees to marry Milind. Dileep comes to know about this and reaches Amrita's office, to talk to her, but Amrita's boss, Mr. Samrat Patel tells Dileep to stay away from Amrita, and avoid hurting her any more.

Because of Amrita, not responding to Dileep's calls and messages, Dileep sends her a letter, asking whom she remembers the most, when she gets up in the morning, when drinking coffee, and when listening to songs online.

Some days after this incident, one day, Dileep's photographer friend, Malhar informs him that Dileep's boss, Vitthal Rajda, after noticing the changes in Dileep's behaviour, ever since, he has met Amrita and ever since, Amrita came in his life, has concluded that Amrita is the reason, due to which, Dileep is not able to concentrate on his work, and therefore, to punish Amrita for this, has taken all the photographs of the Silvassa trip from him, and is going to publish them in tomorrow's all the newspapers, circulated in Mumbai, to defame Amrita.

This makes Dileep tense. However, on the same night, he, along with Malhar secretly manages to enter their boss, Vitthal Rajda's cabin, and is successful in deleting all the pictures from their boss, Rajda's laptop, and with the help of Malhar, his friend, destroys the pen - drive having the back - up, and throws the pen - drive, far away from their office in a manhole.

Dileep, at last decides to make one final attempt of wooing Amrita. He writes all his feelings in a letter, and in the night, puts that letter in Amrita's house's letterbox. That night was none other than the Christmas Eve, as the date was the 24th of December. The next day was the day of the Christmas festival. The next day, on the day of Christmas, when Milind comes to Amrita's home to take Amrita out for coffee, he manages to see Dileep's letter, before Amrita could. When Milind reads the entire letter, he understands that how much Dileep loves Amrita. After meeting Amrita, when he finishes reading the letter, and without informing Amrita about the letter, Milind comes to know that Amrita is not happy with the marriage.

During their coffee date on the Christmas morning, despite asking Amrita a lot, about whether, she is happy with their marriage or not, Amrita chooses to stay quiet, and agreed to Milind, that she is happy with their marriage.

Finally, the day of Milind and Amrita's marriage arrives. The day is none other than the New Year's Day, that is, the 01st of January, 2023. However, one day, prior to their marriage, that is, on the 31st of December, 2022, Milind, in the morning comes to Amrita's house to ask her one last time, if she is happy with the marriage or not.

During this meeting, Milind asks Amrita to say the truth of whom, she really thinks of in her mind. When Amrita cannot answer, Milind tells her that his aim was to see her happy, whether with him or with anyone else. Milind, in this final meeting before the marriage, understands her mind, and agrees to help her meet Dileep, her true love of life.

However, Dileep, who had by now already started giving up on his relationship with Amrita, after not hearing anything from her, even after telling his true and real feelings to Amrita in the letter, which he had put in her mailbox on the day of the Christmas Eve.

After coming to know about Amrita's true love and feelings for Dileep, Milind takes Amrita with her to meet Dileep, and express her true love and feelings, which she had for Dileep. However, they are not able to locate Dileep. Both of them, after failing to get Dileep's where abouts, reaches out to Malhar, Dileep's photographer friend. But, unfortunately, for Milind and Amrita, even Malhar has no idea about the where abouts of Dileep.

Amrita strikes an idea at this point of time. She, along with Milind reaches Amrita ' s Radio Station, and on the radio, she asks the people of Mumbai City to help her find Dileep. She gives the minute details about Dileep on the radio, and asks that, if anyone, anywhere in Mumbai sees or finds him, should contact her on the radio.

However, Milind and Amrita do not get any call from any part of Mumbai about Dileep, and both of them starts losing hope, of whether, Dileep is in Mumbai, or he has left the city.

Finally, after passing of many hours, when the evening sets in, Amrita gets a call from a tea - vendor, Rajubhai Shah, who informs Amrita on the radio that, he is speaking from the Marine Drive, and a man whose descriptions matches with the details given by Milind and Amrita on the radio is sitting at his tea - stall.

Milind and Amrita rush to the spot, where a man like Dileep was sitting, as told by the tea - vendor Rajubhai Shah, and finds the man to be Dileep in real, and actually realise that Raju Patel had recognised Dileep correctly.

Amrita reaches the place and immediately proposes to Dileep by saying that she wants to forget her earlier anger, and wants to start a new relationship with him. Dileep happily accepts the proposal. After accepting the proposal, Dileep thanks Milind for making such a huge sacrifice for him in his life.

After Dileep and Amrita unite, all the three of them-Amrita, Dileep, and Milind look towards the setting sun at the Marine Drive, and realise that they realised the importance of - "true love" on the last day of the year.

All the three decides to celebrate this mega-event in their life by welcoming the new year-2023, and promises to be the best friends for life, and expecting the coming year to be full of love, life, humanity, and compassion.

Hence, to celebrate the momment, and to make it a rememberable one for the entire life, they raise a toast, hailing the victory of - "true love" forever, in every coming second of their life.

Remembering the Works of Baba Saheb Purandare

While going through a graduation course in 'History Of Maharashtra', I found a passing reference to historian Baba Saheb Purandare. Later I got an opportunity to watch the stage play – "Janataraja" written and conceptualized by Babasaheb in a Pune's open theatre. The show was performed by over 300 artists and there were elephants and horses in the playmaking it is comparable to a blockbuster Bollywood movie of today. Such a large number of actors and the presence of animals brought back history to life. The three – hour mega – play revolves around the life and times of the Maratha warrior king Chhatrapati Shivaji Maharaj (a 17th century Maratha king). It was announced during the play that its first show was staged in April 1984, the show has about 1550 editions across the country including the states of Uttar Pradesh and Punjab where its maximum number of shows were staged apart from Maharashtra and also in the USA. I found the show to be a mesmerizing one that brought the 17th century alive on the stage. I was amazed to notice that even without having any formal training in – "Theatrical Art", Baba Saheb had produced his show with grand production – design as well as sound – design inculcated in it. The gorgeousness of production and sound-designs have made the mega show a renowned one and should be a precious heritage for the students of drama and film-making. The grandness in its production -value and my training in Script Writing at FTII, Pune stimulated me to know more about the play as well as about Babasaheb's works. I also noticed that the inspiration for making Janataraja came to him when he watched Roman ballets in open theatres and novelist Agatha Christie's play – "The Mousetrap".

Apart from being a theatre personality of eminence, I found Babasaheb to be a prolific writer and he had mastery in oratory. He dedicated his whole life in the study and penning down the life and times of Shivaji Maharaj. In fact, the mission of his life was to bring Shivaji's life and the way of administering for the knowledge of younger generations. Apart from his number of books, his two-part book – "Raja Shivchhatrapati" is a masterpiece and has sixteen editions, and approximately its five lakh copies have been sold out. His earlier writings which were in scattered forms have been compiled and published in the book – "Thinagya" (which means – 'sparks'). His other works include the books entitled "Kesari", "Lal Mahal", "Savitri", "Phulwanti" etc and a book on the life of Peshwa Narayanrao, the king from Peshwa's lineage who was killed in Pune's Shaniwarwada at a very young age shifting the center of power from Sinhagad, Pune to Kolhapur.

Besides, Babasaheb was a fine orator who used to deliver extempore lectures on the Maratha king in which he used to capture the imagination of his audience. He did not stop his passion for lecturing on – "Shiv Charitra" and kept on holding his lecture series even when he attained the age of 75.

His works which include books authored by him and the lecture series can, at the best, be examined critically by historians and other authorities but they have made Shivaji's life and times significant and live for the present-day youngsters. Our tribute to the versatile playwright, prolific writer, and excellent orator Padma Vibhushan and Maharashtra Bhusan Babasaheb Purandare (99).

Revathi Veeramani: From Running Barefoot to Competing at Tokyo Olympics

Revathi Veeramani lost both her parents when she was only five. She spent her childhood in extreme poverty and ran barefoot in school meets. Despite all these trials and tribulations, Revathi didn't stop chasing her dream of making it big in the sporting arena.

The 23-year-old recently represented India in the 4x400m relay at the ongoing Tokyo Olympics. Her childhood dream has materialised.

EARLY DAYS

Revathi Veeramani

Born in Sakkimangalam village of Madurai, Tamil Nadu, Revathi was brought up by her grandmother after her parents' untimely death. Poverty-stricken as the old lady–a daily wage earner—was, she chose to send Revathi to a nearby school for studies.

In school, she met coach K Kannan who spotted her hidden talent in running and groomed her to be a top athlete. To date, Revathi believes that without the guidance of her childhood coach, she would not have been able to become an international athlete. "All my sporting achievements are due to Kannan sir," she said in a recent interview.

GRADUAL RISE

After participating in several college and district-level events, she shot to the limelight when she clinched gold medals in both 100m and 200m at the Junior Nationals in 2016. Later, she went on to bag a silver medal at the Senior Nationals.

Subsequently, she got selected for a national camp in Patiala which was training athletes for the Olympics. Revathi's reputation grew immensely after she decided to run 400m instead of 100m and 200m following the advice OFA national camp coach, Galina Bukharina.

She has been making rapid strides since then. After performing admirably at the 2019 Asian Championship in Doha, the 23-year-old was able to qualify for the Tokyo Olympics without much difficulty.

At the Olympics, she could not progress beyond the heats but gained experience of competing with the best athletes of the world. With age on her side, the Tamil Nadu girl is expected to get better and bring laurels to the country in the future.

Remembering Nandu Natekar, India's First Badminton Icon

Indian badminton's Grand Old Man, Nandu Natekar, passed away following age-related complications in Pune on July 28. He was 88.

Natekar, a 17-time national badminton champion, was a man of many firsts.

He was the first Indian shuttler to clinch an international title (Malaysia, 1956) and feature among the top-five ranked players in the world (ranked as high as No 3 during his heyday). He was also among the first recipients of the Arjuna Award in 1961.

A file photo of Nandu Natekar showcasing his skills with the racquet.

Natekar or Nandu sir, as he was fondly called, enthralled sportslovers from the 50s and 60s with his deceptive style and stroke perfection at the court. His backhand, in particular, came in for high praise from fans and critics alike.

He though nearly ended up making his career in tennis instead of badminton in his youth.

The legendary shuttler, who grew up in Sangli before his family moved to Mumbai, played both badminton and tennis with consummate ease during his college days.

However, after he lost the final of a junior national championship to future tennis great, Ramanathan Krishanan, he chose to focus entirely on badminton.

Within a short span of time, he carved a niche for himself at the national circuit with his graceful style of play.

A file photo of Nandu Natekar posing with one of many trophies he won during his glittering career.

He was the first Indian to make a mark at the prestigious All England Badminton Championship. In the 1954 edition, he advanced to the quarterfinals before bowing out. His success inspired Prakash Padukone, who finally became the first Indian to win the tournament 28 years later in 1980.

Among his other notable achievements included leading India at the Thomas Cup thrice, bagging men's singles and mixed doubles (with Meena Shaw) titles at Bangkok Kings Cup and representing the country at the 1965 Commonwealth Games in Jamaica.

In 1958, he registered what many claimed his greatest moment of career — a victory over World No 1 Erland Kops en route to the CCI Open crown. He didn't lose his skills even at the age of 47 when he clinched a veteran's doubles title at the All-England Championship.

Natekar's interest in badminton didn't wane after calling time on his professional career. He kept in touch with the young crop of shuttlers including Saina Nehwal and continued to provide them with useful tips on how to take their game to a new level.

A lifelong lover of sports, he would be often seen playing golf in Pune, the city where he lived in his later years. He would be sorely missed.

India & Seven Wonders at Tokyo

The whole of India is in a celebration mood. The reason is India's best-ever performance with a medal tally at seven, including gold in Tokyo Olympics 2020. India's earlier best was at a medal tally of six in the London Olympics 2012, but without any gold medal. The last time, India won a gold medal was way back in Beijing Olympics in 2008 in a 10 m air rifle shooting by Abhinav Bindra. Thus, the country had to wait for a gold medal for 13 long years. The history was rewritten by Haryana Hurricane, Neeraj Chopra when he won a gold medal in Tokyo Olympics 2020 in men's javelin throw. Hence, such a widespread celebration in the country has been overdue. In this story, we have attempted to give an insight into the performances of the seven medal winners in Tokyo.

1. NEERAJ CHOPRA – The golden boy from Haryana, Neeraj Chopra, a Subedar with 04 Rajputana Rifles in the Indian army, became the second Indian to win an individual gold in the Olympics, with a throw of 87. 58 m. Neeraj is independent India's first Indian to win an Olympic medal in the Track and Field event (It was Calcutta born British Indian, Norman Gilbert Pritcharged, who represented India, during British India had won India's first track and field medal at the 1900 Paris Olympics in 200 m race). To achieve the highest success in the javelin throw, full credit also goes to Neeraj's dedication, hard work, and his head coach and former German athlete, Uwe Hohn, who himself had a record javelin throw of 104. 80 m. An achiever and a consistent performer since, 2016, the country has high hopes from 23 – year – old, Neeraj in the coming athletic competitions, including the 2024 Paris Olympics.

2. MIRABAI CHANU – The 26 – year – old weight – lifter from Manipur ended a 21 – year haunt for a medal in weightlifting, when, she bagged a silver medal in 49 kg category weightlifting. In fact, she won her medal on the opening day of the competition (July 24). She lifted a total of 202 kg (87 kg plus 115 kg). Prior to it, she has been a world champion in 2017.

3. RAVI DAHIYA – Ravi Dahiya, another Haryanvi entered into the final of the Men's 57 kg freestyle wrestling in style, showing his great strength and technical knowledge, and won a silver medal. Prior to it, the 23 – year grappler won the Asian championship in 2020.

4. PUSARLA V. SINDHU – PV Sindhu, the ace women shuttler had high hopes of countrymen for a medal in badminton in the Tokyo Olympics. She proved herself right by winning bronze after defeating China's He Bing Jiao by 21–15, 21–13 in two straight sets in just 53 minutes. She became the first Indian woman, and, the

country's second sportsperson to win medals in two consecutive Olympics. Her earlier Olympics medal came when she won a silver at Rio de Janeiro (Brazil) in 2016.

5. MEN'S HOCKEY TEAM – India at one time used to top the world scenario in the field hockey event with a total of 12 medals, including 08 gold, 01 silver, and 03 bronze medals. This was India's third bronze and twelfth hockey medal when India beat Germany 5 – 4 under the able leadership of its halfback, the young Manpreet Singh. It took 41 long years for India to reach the podium in hockey since their gold medal-winning run in the 1980 Moscow Olympics. The country had lost the hope of winning a medal again when Australia routed India, 1 – 7 in their second game itself. Coming back strongly, with strong willpower and superb passes, Manpreet Singh and his men made it to the bronze medal in Tokyo Olympics, 2020.

6. LOVLINA BORGOHAIN – Assam's s Lovlina Borgohain became India's only boxer who bagged a medal – a bronze at Tokyo Olympics. She punched out Turkey's Busenaz Surmeneli in women's 64 – 69 kg Welterweight boxing. Trained at Pune's Army Training Centre, Lovlina became the third Indian boxer after Vijender Singh and M. C. Mary Kom to clinch a medal in Olympic games.

7. BAJRANG PUNIA – A passionate wrestler Bajrang Punia brought the seventh medal in Tokyo Olympics when he bagged a bronze medal after defeating Kazakhstan's Daulet Niyazbekov in men's 65 kg freestyle wrestling. Interestingly, seeing his past performances in the World Championships, there was a high hope of winning a gold in this category from Punia, but his opponent in the semi-final showed better wrestling to defeat Punia, and the 27 – year – old Punia was to be satisfied with a bronze medal in the repechage method.

Thus, the Tokyo Olympics came to an end with a glittering closing ceremony on 08th of August, 2021 with another successful Olympics in Paris in 2024.

Twenty Twinkling Stars in Tokyo Olympics 2020

India had a best-ever performance at the Tokyo Olympics games where they won seven medals including a gold medal for the first time in its sporting history. This article is a SEQUEL to our previous article, "India and seven wonders at Tokyo". Here we introduce 20 future Olympics medal perspectives who have missed the Tokyo Olympics podiums by a whisker in their respective sports. They came close to the glory and adding to the country's medal tally after competing under the highest hopes and pressures against the best available sportspersons on the globe. Although they missed the medals they have become an inspiration for many youngsters looking forward to excelling in their sports. Their spirit, enthusiasm as well as a passion for the sports were worth watching live and therefore these powerhouses of their games were rightly given a rousing welcome after returning back to India. These stars are also being felicitated by different state governments as well as some corporate sector giants befitting to their hard works, efforts, and examples to put in their best.

In subsequent paragraphs we have introduced four such sportspersons and the 16 members of the women's hockey team led by captain Rani Rampal although the list of such sportspersons is much bigger than this :

1. Aditi Ashok (Golf): The 23-year-old Indian golfer from Bengaluru competed against the best golfers of the world, although ranked 200th in the world, she reached till finals of women's individual stroke play of the game. Coming close to clinching a medal she finished only a shot behind Japan's Mone Inami and New Zealand's Lydia Ko to lose the medal. She was only two shots behind the gold medalist Nelly Korda of the USA. Thus, the country lost its chance of winning the first-ever Olympics medal in

golf. She finished fourth and improved her performance at Rio Olympics significantly where she finished 41st. Both the parents are ardent golf lovers, the father being her caddy in Rio and her mother in Tokyo. The country has high hopes of medals from this young performer in upcoming world championships of golf including Paris Olympics of 2024.

2. Deepak Punia (Wrestling): A 22-year lad from Haryana and a JCO in the Indian Army Naib Subedar Deepak Punia is a freestyle wrestler who participated in the 86 kg category. A silver medalist at the 2019 World Wrestling Championships in this category, he also reached comfortably in semi-finals in Tokyo Olympics after defeating Nigerian Ekerekem Agiomor 12 – 01 with his technical superiority over his powerful opponent. In the next match, he was leading 2 – 0 till less than 15 seconds before the final whistle of the fight. His opponent Myles Amine of San Marino overturned his lead of 2 – 0 with

his superior talent which made Amine won the bronze medal in the 86 kg category.

3. Satish Kumar (Boxing): A JCO in the Indian Army and an amateur boxer, Subedar Major Satish Kumar is a bronze medallist of the 2014 Asian Games (Incheon) and a silver medalist of 2018 Commonwealth Games (Gold Coast) in Super Heavyweight category (+ 91 kg). He is the first Indian boxer to take part in the Olympics in the Super Heavyweight category. In the quarter-finals, he lost by 5 – 0 against World and Asian champion Bakhodir Jalolov of Uzbekistan who proved to be a more powerful giant and overmatched Satish Kumar in all the departments. However, Satish Kumar put up a superb performance in spite of blood coming out from his right eye and two cuts he had in his pre-quarter-finals. His punches were so impressive that even his opponent Jalolov showed respect for him by giving a warm hug after the game. With the talent that Satish Kumar has, the country expects a

medal in this category in the coming Paris Olympics 2024.

4. Saurabh Chaudhary (Shooting): A 19-year-old gold medalist at the 2018 Asian Games in 10 m Air Pistol in Indonesia, Saurabh Chaudhary was a strong medal prospect in both the events – individual and mixed team events with his co-shooter, Manu Bhaker in Tokyo. However, in the individual event, this young shooter from Meerut started his first series with a score of a mere 95. Between the 03rd and 05th series he picked up the pace and shot a remarkable 23 tens on the trot and was just an inch before the medal. But subsequently, he could register only 8. 8 in the next 05 points and found himself at the 07th position, just ahead of Kim Mose of South Korea. In the mixed team event, with his accuracy, he scored a perfect 100 in a series twice. However, Bhaker dropped a significant 14 points in total to bring the duo again in the seventh position. Thus, Chaudhary, in spite of his superb talent and skill missed a medal in Tokyo in both events.

5. Women's s Hockey team: Indian women's hockey team squad for the Tokyo Olympics consisted of 16 members, led by 26-year-old captain Rani Rampal. The squad had the goalkeeper Savita Punia, four defenders namely Gurjit Kaur, Deep Grace Ekka, Nikki Pradhan, Udita Duhan, five forwards namely Sharmila Devi, Vandana Katariya, Lalremsiami, Navneet Kaur, Rani Rampal, and six midfielders, namely, Navjot Kaur, Monika Malik, Nisha, Sushila Chanu Pukhrambam, Salima Tete, and Neha Goyal.

The team suffered losses in their first three games in their pool stage but stunned Australia by registering a 1 – 0 win in the quarter-finals. In the semi-finals, they came up with a courageous effort against high-ranked Great Britain's team. The Indian team had entered the semi-finals of the game for the first time stunning hockey pundits. Prior to it, their best was the fourth position in the 1980 Moscow Games. Showing a superb display of hockey against Rio Olympic Champions Great Britain, the team scored

3 – 2 at half-time and surprised everyone by scoring 03 goals in a span of 05 minutes with Gurjit Kaur hitting two goals in 25th and 26th minute and Vandana Katariya hitting one goal in the 29th minute of the game. However, in the second half, the game took a turn in favour of British women who showed superb hockey and scored two goals and changed the match in their favour, thus defeating India by 4 – 3.

This way, the Indian women's hockey team despite not finishing their successful campaign with a medal won the hearts of billions of fans.

Paralympics and Seventeen Gallant Indian Sportspersons

Paralympic Games were in much limelight since they commenced on August 24. Interestingly, the Paralympic Games were founded by Sir Ludwig Guttmann, a Jewish doctor who had started a spinal injury center at the Stoke Mandeville Hospital, England. For faster rehabilitation of 16 injured servicemen and women, he also organised a competition between them in archery which later became a regular part of the rehabilitation center. The competition was named the 'Stoke Mandeville Games' (SMG). Its first edition was organised in July 1948. The SMG later became the Paralympic Games. The first Paralympic Games were hosted by Rome (Italy) in 1960. 23 countries with about 400 athletes participated in these games. In order to give these games an international character, the International Paralympic Committee (IPC) was formed in 1989 as the Global governing body of the Paralympic movement.

These games are now held after every 4 years. They succeed in the Summer Olympic Games and are staged by the host country of the Olympic Games of that year. These games are organised jointly by the IPC and a few non – para national federations. For example, table tennis is governed by the TT Federation of India.

Based on the types and extents of the disability of participants, classifications of para-players are done. Classifications, which are done by qualified classifiers, play an important role. Players compete against those players who have a similar level of ability. Based on the disabilities of players, each sport is also classified. A sport can have more than one classification. For example, table tennis has 10 classifications. There are 10 different types of physical impairments. They include orthopedic issues, nerve problems, and problems of the central nervous system. Even vision and intellectual impairments are also included in these deficiencies.

The year 2020 para – games were staged in Japan, which is the only country so far that has hosted these games twice – In 2020 and in 1964. For the first time, Badminton and Taekwondo made entry into these games held in Tokyo. Another feature of the Tokyo Para Olympic Games was the participation of a refugee paralympic team led by a US Paralympian, Ileana Rodriguez, herself a refugee. In total 4403 para-athletes participated in the Tokyo Paralympics. This included 2550 male and 1853 female athletes. The TV viewership also surpassed the previous number of viewers having a 4. 10 billion cumulative audiences set at Rio 2016. In the 2020 Tokyo games, 22 sports with 539 events were held between 163 participating countries. The above data shows the popularity of these games not only among the participants but also in the TV viewers.

India started taking part in Paralympic Games in 1972 and the total medals won by the Indian contingent since then have been 12 including 4 medals at the Rio Games 2016. In Tokyo, India competed in 9 sports with 54 athletes. The best-ever Olympics Games for India just went by and there was a curiosity among sports lovers whether Indian Paralympians could surpass the tally of seven medals won by the Indian Olympians. The gallant Indian Paralympians have proved their supremacy by winning a significant number of19 medals (5 Gold, 8 Silver, 6 Bronze) at Tokyo. What a significant rise in medal tally from the previous Rio Olympics! The full credit goes to our seventeen valorous para Olympians. With 12 packed days of sporting actions, the games came to an end on September 5, 2021, which were held under tight security due to COVID – 19 restrictions.

Paralympics and Seventeen Gallant Indian Sportspersons

This article is a sequel to our article on Indian Paralympians. Here we put forward a description of the games and performance of the seventeen proud medal winners, in brief, in Tokyo Paralympic Games 2020 (their names appear in alphabetical orders in all the three types of medals) :

A. GOLD MEDALLISTS – There have been the following 5 Gold Medallists,

1. AVANI LEKHARA – The 19-year golden girl from Jaipur is a para rifle shooter. She is not only a gold medallist in 10 m air rifle shooting but she also clinched a bronze medal in the 50 m air rifle shooting. For her gold, she defeated reigning champion

Zhang Cuiping of China. She bagged her bronze by scoring 445.90 m. She earned the distinction of being the FIRST Indian woman to win 2 medals in the same edition of the Paralympic Games.

2. KRISHNA NAGAR- A promising para shuttler also from Jaipur, Krishna Nagar won the gold medal in men's singles badminton SH 6 event by defeating Hong Kong's Chu Man Kai in three sets 21 – 17, 16 – 21, 21 – 17. He showed his superiority in backhand returns.

3. MANISH NARWAL – 19-year-old Manish from Faridabad is a para shooter in an air pistol event. He won his gold medal in mixed P 4 50 m air pistol shooting SH 1. His winning shot was 218. 20, which is a paralympic world record.

4. PRAMOD BHAGAT – Pramod Bhagat's gold medal in men's singles badminton came when he defeated convincingly Great Britain's Daniel Bethill Margive in two straight sets 21 – 14, 21 – 17. This young

man from Odisha had full control over the game right from the beginning.

5. SUMEET ANTIL – A F 64 men's javelin thrower Sumeet bagged his gold medal by improving his own world record of 62.88 m almost by six meters. He started his throw with a world record of 66. 90 m and bettered it twice in his second throw (68.08 m) and in his fifth throw (68.55 m). The world record holder Sumeet Antil is from Sonepat.

B. SILVER MEDALLISTS – There have been the following 8 Silver Medallists,

1. BHAVINABEN PATEL – The table tennis player from Mehsana, a 34-year-old paddler scripted history by becoming the first Indian table tennis player to secure a medal in Paralympics. She had a scintillating win over World Number 5 Borislava Peric Rankovic of Serbia in the semi-final of Women's s single class IV event. She won her quarter-final in just 18 minutes.

2. DEVENDRA JHAJHARIA – Two times gold medal-winning javelin throw veteran, Devendra (40) from Churu, Rajasthan has completed the hat-trick of winning the medals at the Paralympic games. His first gold was at Athens games 2004 with a world record of 62. 15 m, the second gold came at Rio Paralympics 2016 with a world record of 63. 97 m which is higher than his own Athens World Record. At Tokyo Paralympics 2020 he won his third medal (silver) with his personal best throw of 64. 35 m which is better than his Rio mark (javelin throw was not a part of paralympic games held at Beijing (2008) and at London (2012)).

3. MARIYAPPAN THANGAVELU – The 25-year-old high jumper in T 63 event from Tamil Nadu won a silver medal with his best high jump of 1.86 m, which is his second Paralympics medal. An Arjuna awardee (2017) and also a Padma Shri in 2017, he has been a gold medallist of the Rio Paralympics 2016.

4. NISHAD KUMAR – A student of physical education from Punjab, Nishad was jointly declared a silver medallist along with US high jumper Dallas Wise by clearing 2.06 m which is an Asian record set by himself in Dubai where he clinched a gold medal. A small-town resident of Una (HP) now eyes to repeat his Dubai performance at the next paralympic games in Paris, 2024.

5. PRAVEEN KUMAR – The 18-year-old Delhi University student competed in the men's T 44 high jump event at Tokyo and won silver by climbing 2. 07 m which is his personal best. The gutsy Praveen achieved this milestone in spite of getting confined to his room for almost 45 days owing to COVID – 19 in April this year.

6. SINGHRAJ ADHANA – A proud owner of two medals – silver in P 4 mixed 50 m air pistol shooting SH 1 event has a total of 216. 70 points and a bronze in P 1 men's 10 m air pistol SH 1 event with 216. 80 points. The 39 year – old Singhraj from Haryana

picked up this sport only four years ago. But with his determination and belief, he quickly climbed the success ladder.

7. SUHAS L. YATHIRAJ – A rare combination of an administrator and a sports person, Suhas hails from Karnataka. Currently a district magistrate at Noida, UP Suhas clinched a silver medal in badminton and is a first-ever IAS officer to win a medal in paralympics. He won the silver after he lost the final against France's Lucas Mazur in the men's singles badminton event SL 4 by 21–15, 17–21, 15–21 in spite of winning the first set.

8. YOGESH KATHUNIA – A 24 year–old Yogesh clinched a silver medal in the men's discussion throw F 56 event with the best distance of 44. 38 m in his sixth and last attempt. A commerce graduate from New Delhi, he created a world record in his first-ever international competition in 2018 held in Berlin.

C. BRONZE MEDALLISTS – There are six bronze medallists including Avani Lekhara and Singhraj Adhana who have won respectively gold and a silver apart from the bronze medal. The four remaining bronze medallists are as follows –

1. HARVINDER SINGH – World Number 23 archer Harvinder won India's first medal in archery in paralympic games in the form of a bronze medal. Playing men's individual recurve open event, 29 year – old archer scored a perfect 10 in the shoot-off beating Kim Min Su of South Korea with scores 6 – 5 in a closely fought contest to earn his medal. He lost his semi-final to Kevin Mather of the US with a score 4 – 6. A master's and a doctoral degree holder in Economics and a resident of a small town Kaithal of Haryana, he has a passion for the sports of archery hopes to improve his performance in forthcoming international games.

2. MANOJ SARKAR – A gold medalist at the 2016 Asian Championship held in Beijing, shuttler Manoj Sarkar from Uttarakhand won a bronze in men's single badminton

SL 3 category by beating Japan's Daisuke Fujihara in two straight sets – 22 – 20, 21 – 13. His first set was a nail-biting clash while the second set was an easy cakewalk for him.

3. SHARAD KUMAR – Muzaffarpur's Sharad Kumar became Bihar's first-ever Paralympic medallist when he won a bronze medal in the F 42 category of men's high jump in the Tokyo Paralympics Games.

4. SUNDAR SINGH GURJAR – The 25 year – old Sundar from Jaipur clinched a bronze medal finishing behind Devendra Jhajharia in the men's javelin throw F 46 final with his best throw of 64. 10 m. This way India captured two medals out of three in the men's javelin F 46 event in the Tokyo Paralympics – a rare achievement in international games.

NOTE – Discuss thrower Vinod Kumar won a bronze medal in the F 52 category with a throw of 19. 91 m but his classification in the F 52 category was challenged by other competitors resulting in Vinod Kumar losing his bronze medal after being found ineligible in disability classification assessment by the competition panel.

The above lion-hearted sportspersons have proven that mere physical disability cannot be a hurdle for achieving a target but it can be compensated with mental toughness and willpower. These young leaders have also given a message to the society to change its outlook towards 'Divyangs'. It should be our duty not to applaud their performances only after four years but to hail them consistently. Our salute to them.

The Indian Premier League

The Indian Premier League (IPL) is a cricket tournament played every year in our country where the game of cricket is like a religion having an uncountable number of followers spread over the entire country. IPL is the brainchild of Mr. Lalit Modi, ex-vice president of the Board of Cricket Control of India (BCCI) having a format exactly parallel to England's English Premier League (EPL) in football and America's National Basketball Association (NBA) in basketball. Founded by the BCCI in 2007, IPL is a professional 20 – 20 format cricket league played between eight teams usually from March to May every year. The year 2020 was an exception, due to the surge of COVID – 19, when IPL was organised from 19th September to 10th November in the United Arab Emirates (UAE)

although the matches were initially scheduled in India like every year.

There have been thirteen seasons of IPL so far and currently, the 14th season is underway. In fact, the fourteenth season took off as per the schedule from April 09, 2021, and was played till May 02, 2021 but was to be postponed till September 18, 2021, due to the second wave of the pandemic. The season was re-started from September 19 in the UAE in a bio-secure bubble in which matches are being held at a centralised site with strict quarantine and safety protocols. In part – 1 of IPL, 29 league matches were played and the remaining 31 matches are being held from September 19, the final being scheduled on October 15.

The first season of IPL was started in April 2008 in New Delhi in a grand inaugural ceremony. The genesis of IPL originated from India's victory at the 2007 20 – 20 World Cup. Bubbling with the enthusiasm that emerged from this victory, BCCI announced a franchise-based 20 – 20 cricket tournament.

Eight teams were decided to participate in the tournament through an auction held in January 2008. The winning bidders were given the team's ownership and the cities to which they belonged were called the base cities of the teams. The names of the teams include the names of the base cities/states. For example, the team DC has its base in Delhi. Likewise, the eight participating teams were – CSK (Chennai Super Kings), DC (Delhi Capitals), KKR (Kolkata Knight Riders), MI (Mumbai Indians), PK (Punjab Kings), RCB (Royal Challengers Bangalore), RR (Rajasthan Royals), and SRH (Sunrisers Hyderabad). Since its commencement in 2008, the above eight teams are participating in every IPL season except for the teams CSK and RR which were suspended on the charges of match-fixing and betting. During their suspensions in the years 2016 and 2017, the two new teams namely the GL (Gujarat Lions) and the RPS (Rising Pune Supergiants) were inducted. However, the team CSK and RR were taken back in the IPL- fold when their suspensions were revoked in 2018. The two new teams – the GL and the RPS were dropped. In the year 2011, ten teams were allowed to participate and in 2012, nine teams played the tournament. Except for these two years, only eight teams participated every year in the tournament.

All the eight teams acquire the players in either of the three ways – annual player auction, trading players with other teams, or signing replacements for unavailable players. Players sign- up for the auction and set their base prices. During the auction, the franchise that bids the highest for a player is said to have bought that player. As per the rule, a team can have a maximum of four cricketers from outside the country.

Each team plays with all the remaining teams in the league- phase in a round-robin format. 56 matches are played at league levels and the top four teams in the points- tally qualify for the play-offs. The winner of the first two teams, one and two, gets direct entry into the IPL final. This match is called Qualifier round match number 1. The last two teams, number three and number four, play against each other and the match is called the Eliminator match. The loser of Qualifier match number 1 plays with the winner of the Eliminator match and this match is called Qualifier match number 2. The IPL final is played between the winners of Qualifier match number 1 and Qualifier match number 2. This way there are 60 matches played in every IPL and the entire duration of IPL is spread over almost sixty days. Out of the thirteen seasons played so far, team Mumbai has won five times leaving behind teams Chennai and Kolkata who have won the IPL respectively three and two times. The teams Delhi, Punjab, and Bangalore are yet to win any IPL.

The IPL has been designed to entice an entirely new generation of sports -lovers into the grounds. It attracts a young fan- base which includes ladies, children, and even Indian diasporas. It not only promotes cricket in India but also grooms young and budding cricketers from every nook and corner of the country. IPL provides a platform for young Indian cricketers to play with international star cricketers thereby it becomes a training ground for them.

The impact of IPL is so wide and powerful that during almost two months of the match- days of IPL, there is a definite decline in the TRP's (Telly Rating Points) of TV serials, reality shows, as well as TV news channels. Even the filmmakers avoid releasing their films during IPL. IPL has emerged as an excellent example of professionalism, marketing, and advertisement. Inspired by the IPL formula, a number of other leagues involving games like kabaddi, badminton, hockey, etc have come up with more spectators and more revenue.

The details of the other features of IPL games and its rules include expansions and terminations, players acquisition squads and salaries, team composition rules, prize money, awards, title sponsorships are not discussed here to avoid coming to this article under editor's scissor for exceeding its length.

Chennai Super Kings (CSK): The King of IPL – 2021

The day of mega cricket carnival, IPL came to an end on October 15 after interesting 56 matches between eight teams and the team CSK convincingly lifted the coveted IPL trophy, 20 crore INR, and its dashing player Ruturaj Gaikwad getting crowned with orange cap for scoring highest runs (635) in the tournament.

This IPL will be remembered for its two firsts. For the first time in its thirteen years of history, IPL had been played in two parts – part – 1 in India (April 09 to May 02, 2021) and part – 2 in UAE (September 19 to October 15, 2021). Secondly, the IPL final was played between the weakest opponent so far (Kolkata Knight Riders, KKR) and the mighty CSK. Sadly for the cricket lovers across pan

India who liked to see a tough bat-ball fight for the craved IPL cup. The result of the IPL final became anybody's guess in favour of team CSK. There was a complete mismatch in the IPL final.

During the 2020 IPL, CSK's performance was a complete heart-break for its fans. The team had failed to qualify even for the playoffs and had finished seventh in the points tally. Such was a gloom over the CSK performance in 2020 IPL that no one had expected a better performance from them in 2021. But with their determination, the team silenced their critics and became the first team to qualify for the IPL 2021 playoffs. Its captain MS Dhoni (lovingly called Mahi) led the team from the front and he kept his words made in the last IPL. In his own words which he had said after getting knocked out from the playoffs race in a horrifying last year's IPL season – "we will come back stronger, that is what we are known for".

CSK won 09 from 14 matches they had played before playoffs and thrashed Delhi

Capitals (DC) in the Qualifier Match No. 1 to enter directly in the final of the tournament for a record eighth time. This match had its thrilling end as Dhoni, playing a captain's knock, scored 18 runs in his six-ball innings by hitting 3 fours and 1 six and snatched the victory from the jaws of defeat of his team against DC – the number 1 team amongst the four teams of playoffs. Before Dhoni's arrival, all the viewers were waiting for DC to enter the final but Dhoni's short innings of 18 runs turned the table in favour of CSK. On the other hand, the comparatively weaker team and team number 4 in the playoffs could manage to reach the final for the third time. They defeated the Royal Challengers Bangalore (RCB) in the Eliminator round, led by national captain Virat Kohli. The team DC was later knocked out of the tournament after losing Qualifier match number 1 to team CSK and Qualifier match number 2 to team KKR. The players who contributed superbly in the victory saga were, apart from Ruturaj Gaikwad, Faf Du Plessis (South Africa), Robin Uthappa, and Moeen Ali (England).

Dhoni is now in for a national cause when BCCI appointed him 'mentor' for the Indian national cricket team in the T 20 World Cup, commencing from October 17, 2021, in the UAE. Indeed a wise decision was taken by the BCCI, seeing the cricketing excellence of 'Captain Cool' Dhoni. It is truly said that – "Dhoni jaisa koi nahin".

Dismal Performance of Team India: T20 Cricket World Cup

Team India landed in UAE for the T20 cricket world cup 2021 as one of the toughest contenders for the cup under the captaincy of Virat Kohli and with a squad of 15 promising cricketers, legendary chief coach Ravi Shastri and cricketing icon MS Dhoni as the mentor of the team.

India played its first match with Pakistan on October 24. As well -known, the match between teams India and Pakistan is played not only by these two teams but the entire cricket-crazy populace from the two countries also watch the match glued to their TV sets with jumpy breath. India's second match was scheduled against New Zealand (Kiwis) on October 31. Prior to these two matches,

India defeated two mighty teams – England and Australia in the warming-up matches. However, due to a number of factors that we will discuss later in this article, India was beaten mercilessly by both Pakistan and Kiwis. The defeats were not only shameful for a strong team like India but it almost shut the door for team India to enter the semi-finals of the tournament. Although some cricket pundits are of the view that India might get entry into semi-finals by a few permutations and combinations, whose discussion will be out of place for this article.

After the two stunning defeats of team India, the Indian cricket lovers celebrated team India's comfortable win over Afghanistan and Scotland with a washed-out smile on their faces. India also improved its net run rate (NRR) marginally after the two wins.

JAB TEAM INDIA MET TEAM PAKISTAN – Including this match India has played six T 20 cricket tournaments for the world cup with Pakistan. Except for this match, India has emerged victorious in all five matches. The first encounter was at Johannesburg in 2007, which India won by 5 runs. In the second encounter which was a day-night match at the Oval in 2009, India won by9 wickets with 18 balls remaining. In the third match held at Colombo in 2012, India won by 8 wickets with 18balls remaining. In the fourth match held at Dhaka in 2014, India won by 7 wickets with 9 balls remaining. The fifth match held at Kolkata in 2016 was also won by India by 6 wickets with 13 balls remaining. In the latest sixth encounter held at Dubai, India lost poorly by all the 10 wickets with 13balls remaining. This was the biggest record- defeat of Team India in any world cup fixtures. Pakistan's young speedster Shaheen Afridi broke the nerves of the Indian batting lineup by sending Indian star batters Rohit Sharma, KL Rahul, and Virat Kohli back to the pavilion by giving away just 31runs. The fall of wickets of Sharma and Rahul in the early overs of the match was enough to demoralize the rest of the Indian batters. The two balls of Afridi on which Sharma and Rahul went out were worth watching. In fact, the duo could not understand at all the stunning deliveries which got them out. The sole effort of Kohli from one end was not enough as from the other end Indian batters kept falling like playing cards. In Pakistan's Innings, Indian star seamers Md. Shami and B. Kumar were beaten so badly that most of the spectators left the stands for their homes. It was an outright victory of Team Pakistan when Pakistan's opening pair of Md. Rizwan and Baber Azam outplayed Indian bowling and fielding. Team Pakistan's performance has been really praise-worthy.

JAB TEAM INDIA MET TEAM NEW ZEALAND – Prior to this world cup, the teams India and New Zealand have met twice in the T20 cricket world cup. India could not defeat the Kiwis in either of the two matches. In the inaugural edition of the T20 cricket world cup held in South Africa in 2007, Kiwis was the only team that defeated India in spite that India won the world cup. In the 2016 clash between the two countries held in India, New Zealand scored 126 runs and in its reply, Indian batting had collapsed for just 79 runs after losing all the wickets. In the ongoing world cup, India showed a pathetic display of their batting and could score only 110 runs for 7 wickets in the allotted 20 overs. Replying to this small score, the NZ batters comfortably reached the target in just 14.3 overs by scoring 111runs with only 2 wickets loss. India lost the match by 8 wickets with 33balls remaining.

Victory and defeat are parts of any sporting event but losing matches the way India lost by surrendering itself in front of the opponent was unjustified. There seems to be a number of factors for India's disappointing performance in this world cup. Some of them have been poor team selection, dependency on the IPL -brand of Indian cricketers like Yadav, Kishen, Pant, and meddling with the batting orders. Players selected for the national team from IPL need to be taught the basics of batting for playing in international matches. They should be categorically counseled and told the difference between standards of IPL and international tournaments. IPL is for amusement and entertainment while matches such as the world cups are played for national pride. BCCI also behaved strangely by announcing a new chief coach for team India and starting the process of IPL auction for the year 2022 while the world cup is still on. The two announcements could have been delayed till the end of the world cup.

The time has come that a robust training camp is organised for young cricketers selected for the national team before the commencement of such tournaments. Restrictions should also be imposed on the senior cricketers on their shooting schedule of the endorsements at least before 2 months of such matches. Corporate culture needs to be brought into sports also starting with cricket. After all, the cricketers are paid so handsomely for such matches and the money, of course, comes indirectly from poor tax payer's pockets.

T20 Cricket World Cup 2021: A Brief Survey

After almost a month of mega cricket event, the tournament T20 I World Cup 2021 came to an end on November 14 leaving behind many broken-hearts, unforgettable cricketing -shots, unmatched score-chasing, unimaginably brilliant and dropped catches, and top of it sweet and sour memories of nonstop 26 days of cricket of international standards. It mesmerized the cricket fans from all the cricket-playing nations.

The International Cricket Council (ICC) has been doing a commendable job of promoting the game of cricket in those countries where the game is not so popular. It provides entry to some of such countries in every T-20 I and makes their two groups and picks up the best 2-2 teams from both groups and inducts them into the main WC fold. In this edition, Sri Lanka, Namibia, Ireland Netherlands (GroupA) and Scotland, Bangladesh, Oman, Papua New Guinea (Group B) played their league matches till October 22, and based on their points tally Sri Lanka and Namibia from Group A and Scotland with Bangladesh from Group B made their entry into the main tournament which started from October 23. The total number of countries which clashed for the prestigious World Cup was 12 (called super 12) – 4 from above novice nations (called associate nations) and 8 registered test playing nations.

HIGHLIGHTS OF SUPER 12 MATCHES

All 12 nations in the super 12 were put into 2 groups-Group 1 (England, Australia, South Africa, Sri Lanka, West Indies, and Bangladesh) and Group 2 (Pakistan, New Zealand, India, Afghanistan, Namibia, and Scotland). This stage of the tournament started with the match between two tough teams of Group 1-Aussies and Protease. As expected, the match was so closely finished-one that it was difficult to know the result till the last over, a beauty of T-20 games. The second match was a cakewalk for Britishers as they snatched the victory from the jaws of West Indians early by bowling their batters out cheaply. In the fifth match, Afghanistan surprised everyone and built up a huge score of 190 runs which was difficult for Scotland to reach and they were bundled out just for 60 runs to face the biggest defeat of the tournament. In match no. 11, West Indians won a thriller against Bangladesh by mere 3 runs giving the viewers a breath-stopping end. In match no 14 between England and Australia, the Britishers thrashed the Kangaroos with aid of electrifying batting of Buttler by 8 wickets and signaled themselves as the possible winner of the cup. The ONLY century of this world cup came in match no 17 which was played between England and Sri Lanka when Buttler hit 101*all along the ground making the way for Britishers to register an easy win. India's fate was hanging on the outcome of the match no.28 between New Zealand and Afghanistan.

The Kiwis silenced the cricket pundits of their childish permutations and combinations in favour of India when they beat Afghanistan comfortably by a big margin of 8 wickets. This result made the early exit of India from the World Cup 2021 even without reaching the semi-final stage. The top 2 teams from Group-1 -England and Australia and the top two teams from Group 2- Pakistan and New Zealand entered the semi-finals.

INDIA'S EARLY EXIT

After the two humiliating defeats of team India against Pakistan and New Zealand, India's chances of reaching the semi-final had diminished. Much has been written and spoken about these two defeats in print and electronic media (see also our write-up on the topic in the November 7 issue of this journal). India then played against Afghanistan, Scotland, and Namibia, the 3 newbies of the tournament of its group. As expected, India won all the 3 matches easily as there was no match of team India with them. However, for academic purposes and record books, India won three matches out of its 5 league matches! KL Rahul and Rohit Sharma added one-half century each in their kitties by playing against those teams which are learning the game of cricket. It was for anyone, seeing the standards of top teams, Australia, England, South Africa, and New Zealand that Indian batters, especially youngsters, stand nowhere in front of them. BCCI should think of getting them coached by the likes of Ricky Ponting, Simon Katich, and such other specialists who are most of the time available in India. BCCI should also think of conducting the IPL every alternate year as the cash-rich IPL has been a good cause of distraction for young cricketers who want to mint money in the shortest period of timekeeping aside the national pride.

THE FIRST SEMI-FINAL

A real setback for England which was seen as one of the finalists of the tournament as the Kiwis defeated England with the help of super exciting innings of Mitchell(72*),who hit 4 fours and 4 sixes, Conway (46)who hit 5 fours and one six and pinch hitter Neesham who scored 27 in just 11 deliveries with 3 sixes and one four. The Kiwis outsmarted England's score of 166/4 in their allotted 20 overs by scoring 167 in 19 overs. A splendid performance by the Kiwis batters by their cracker-bursting performance.

THE SECOND SEMI-FINAL

This match was a reminder to Team Pakistan of the popular saying that "the catches win the matches". In his over-enthusiasm and aggressive approach, Hasan Ali ran ahead of a high catch given by Kangaroo's stumper Wade and dropped his catch on the third ball of the 19th over off star bowler of the tournament Shaheen Afridi. Wade utilised this opportunity and hit three consecutive sixes off the last three balls of Afridi. This sparkling display of batting by Wade did the impossible task of taking Aussies into the final as the Kangaroos needed 18 runs in just nine deliveries. Other super hitters with their bats were Warner (49), Marsh (28), and Stoinis(40). Although set a safe target of 177 by Team Pakistan, Aussies achieved it in 19 overs and Team Pakistan was denied its entry into the final by the "will not give away till the last ball" approach of the fighter batters of Australia. A real thriller of the tournament.

THE GREAT FINALE

For the final of the tournament, the Kangaroos locked horns with the Kiwis at Dubai International Stadium. There was great enthusiasm in the cricket lovers to see a big clash between the two toughest teams of the tournament. On the contrary, the first 10 overs of the game were dull and slow when Kiwis started playing first. Even the power play was not fully utilised to gear up the score and it looked as if the final will be a low-scoring match. The score was only 57 runs in 10 overs. The credit goes to Aussies pacer Hazlewood who claimed three valuable wickets of the Kiwis using his perfect in and off cutters. He gave away only 16 runs in making the Kiwis camp tense. But kudos to captain Williamson who by playing a captain's knock accelerated the innings and made 85 runs in just 48 balls and he reached a milestone of this World Cup by making the fastest half-century only in just 32 balls. New Zealand set a target of 173 runs. Australians hammered the Kiwis pace battery and moved ahead with 2 big partnerships. First, between Warner and Marsh (92) and then between Maxwell and Marsh (66). The match became one-sided and Kangaroos won the tournament by 8 wickets making the way for their maiden World Cup victory. Like on two earlier occasions, New Zealand could not clinch the trophy even after reaching the final for the third time. For his aggressive performance with the bat throughout the tournament, Aussies Warner was adjudged as the Player of the tournament.

Lessons From Recent Tour of Team New Zealand's Cricket Series

After a disgraceful defeat of Team India against Team New Zealand, which became the reason for Team India's early ouster from the recently concluded World Cup at the league level, there was a big solace for Indian cricket lovers when Team India confidently and aggressively crushed the same Team New Zealand in both the formats – T-20 I and test cricket played in India after the World Cup. Team India washed out the three T-20 I match series by 3 – 0 and had a clean sweep of the two-match test series by 1 – 0. The result of the test series would also have been 2 – 0 but the heroic performances of the two India – born players of Kiwis – Number 10 down Ajaz Patel and the batter Rachin Ravindra prevented

Team India from achieving the landmark. Both the players kept Indian bowlers longing by bravely playing 60 balls without getting out till the end of the game and thus the first test match was a tame draw.

The above T-20 I matches compel one to analyse what went wrong in the T-20 I World Cup match held at Dubai where the same team Kiwis thrashed Team India giving a blow to the Indian cricket lovers. In this match, Team India batters including it's hit-man Rohit Sharma (14) and stylish captain Virat Kohli (09) became helpless against New Zealand bowlers. The Indian bowlers were also no different in that match and they were at loss and equally helpless against Kiwi batters. There is no point in talking about the performances of Ishaan Kishan (04), Rishabh Pant (12), and Shardul Thakur (00) who have little or no experience of playing international cricket on foreign soil. Of course, they have mesmerised our selectors and got selected by hitting a few high-rise shots in IPL, standards of matches of which are no secret. The show-off of Pant where he hits a ball and releases his one hand after hitting to give an impression that he is capable of hitting a ball with one hand proves my point. In the subsequent paragraphs, I have tried to find out the reasons behind the two contrary results – the disappointing defeat against Team New Zealand at foreign soil in the World Cup and a colourful victory against the same Team New Zealand at the Indian soil: –

A. Possible ongoing cold war between Rohit Sharma and Virat Kohli took a toll on Team India's performance in the first two matches of the World Cup. Interestingly Sharma hits three consecutive fifties in T 20 I against Team New Zealand in India when Kohli was not a part of the playing squad in which Sharma captained Team India and then Sharma abstains himself from the test series when Kohli comes back as a captain in the second test.

B. BCCI gets our pitches in India slow and spin-friendly thereby preventing our batters to get used to of playing the seamers who are the dominating parts of any good international team. BCCI also does not take pain in sponsoring young Indian batters to be a part of English counties for their exposure.

C. Keeping two swords in one sheath – BCCI chose to send MS Dhoni as the mentor of team India for the World Cup along with its chief coach Ravi Shastri. Although it was done with good intentions it was proved like keeping two swords in one sheath. Perhaps it was an embarrassing situation for the legend Shastri. Their collective decisions about the batting orders, selection of bowlers for the squad were proved to be disastrous. Who can forget the inclusion of Varun Chakravarthy in the crucial match against the Kiwis after his dismal performance against Team Pakistan and changing the batting orders of Sharma and Jadeja and letting Kishen open the inning in the match against New Zealand in the World Cup?

D. Unutilising the powerplay – Probably Team India was the only team whose batters did not utilise the first six overs of the powerplay to build up a good start in the first two matches of the World Cup. Our batters lack this skill.

E. Negative effect of IPL – In recent times, the selection of our national team has been heavily influenced by the performances of players in IPL matches instead of focussing on their overall performances in a season.

Let us hope that BCCI takes note of these points and in the future, we will be able to watch good cricket from Team India in prestigious tournaments like World Cups.

Exemplary Cricket From Indian Petals

Indian Under – 19 cricket team gave cricket lovers a perfect new year gift on February 6, 2022, when they not only lifted the coveted ICC U – 19 World Cup trophy for the fifth time but they also made their dominance in the entire tournament by winning all the six matches they had played, a rare feat indeed. It was a sweet coincidence that the day Team South Africa (Sr.) was celebrating the Freedom Test series – win over Team India (Sr.), Indian colts defeated the Proteas (Jr.) in their opening game.

In this 14th edition of the game, 16 teams had participated including mighty Australia and England and was held in West Indies. The 50 over format games and round-robin and knockout format tournament was led by 19-year-old Delhi's lad Yash Dhull. With his sensible and controlled shots all along the ground, Dhull became the third Indian captain of hitting a century in the U – 19 WC after Virat Kohli and Unmukt Chand. His heroics of hitting a century in the semi-final against Australia guaranteed a place for Team India in the final. Before this WC Dhull also led Team India in U – 16 and U – 19 Asia Cups. Throughout his captaincy in this World Cup Dhull did not let pressure affect him and kept himself calm like India's s ex-captain – cool MS Dhoni. Many cricket experts find a resemblance in his game with that of KL Rahul. With this victory, the Indian colts became instrumental in shedding away the gloom created over Indian cricket due to three consecutive defeats of Team India (Sr.) – WC 2021, the Freedom Test series trophy, and T – 50 series with South Africa, all played at foreign soils.

Before writing about the players who made this victory possible, let us have a closer look at the final clash of the tournament.

#. THE FINAL – It was played at Antigua and was the sixth match of the tournament for Team India. The opponent was England which has dashing and hitter batters and quality speedsters. Bowling first, Indian bowlers stunned the cricketing community by restricting England to 189. At one stage miracle was done by the Indian pacers when they contained the top 7 English batters to a meager 91. However, due to the sole effort of James Rew (95 off 116 balls), England's s innings could reach a total of 189. Chasing

190 Team India got a blow when its highest run-scorer for India (278) opener Raghuvanshi got out for a duck in the very first over. However, with the steady knocks of Nishant Sindhu (50*) and Rasheed (50), the Indian victory inched closer. Stumper Dinesh Bana finished the final in style when he hit two consecutive sixes to reach the target and sealed the match for India taking India to its fifth U – 19 World Cup title.

Indian colts played all their six matches as one unit under the able leadership of skipper Dhull. Unlike Team India (Sr.), this team's enthusiasm, passion, and do-or-die approach were the main highlights of Team India's s performance. The mammoth 204 run partnership between Dhull and Rasheed, magical spells of left-arm orthodox spinner Vicky Ostwal (av. – 13. 33), the spectacular shots of Bawa all along the ground, and cuts, drives, and hooks of captain Dhull have all mesmerized the Indian sports lovers during the tournament.

With the proper guidance, these petals can blossom into cricketers of international standards and they will serve Indian cricket for a long time to come.

The IPL Auction

During my childhood, I was told about cattle auction melas in which cattle from nearby places were brought to a centralized place called a sale barn in every bigger district for their sale and purchase. Later I realized that we Indians are very fond of different melas. To name a few are – Magh Mela (Prayagraj), Rath Yatra Mela (Puri), Chatushringi Mela (Pune), and many more. Readers, in this, write up we will examine a mela of the 21st century wherein cricketers are auctioned and "sold". Those who "purchase" such players are called franchises. Crores of rupees change hands in such melas. Few crores of rupees are also passed on to foreign countries while purchasing overseas cricketers of these countries. This mela has been on since 2008 and this year it was organized on February 12 and 13 in Bengaluru. Let us have a brief look at the IPL 2022 auction.

This year a total of 590 players including 370 Indian and 220 overseas players were auctioned for 10 teams which would be a part of the IPL 2022 tournament tentatively beginning from March 26. Australians topped the list with 47 players who got registered for the auction. Day 1 of the auction saw 74 players getting bought by respective franchises while Day 2 saw a little faster auction process during which 130 players were bought. A total of 204 players were sold with all the 10 teams including 67 overseas players. The total amount for which these players were purchased was gobsmacking 551 crores. Out of this more than 200 crores were spent on cricketers from abroad. The highest price to a foreign cricketer was spent on purchasing Britisher Liam Livingstone (Rs. 11.5 crores) while the highest price to an Indian cricketer was spent on purchasing a wicket-keeper batter Ishan Kishan (Rs. 15.25 crores).

Out of the 10 teams, Punjab-based team PBKS spent the highest amount of Rs. 72 crores in the auction. Next to Kishan was all-rounder Deepak Chahar who was purchased at a whopping price of Rs. 14 crores. In the auction process, several cricketers made a huge windfall. Some of them were amazed to know there – "worth". A few of them were embarrassed to know their high purchase prices.

Deepak Chahar was one of them. He did not want to be purchased at such a flamboyant price. There is another aspect of this story. Players coming from BPL families who are unable to make a place for themselves in their state-level teams despite their cricketing talents are purchased at a good price in the IPL auctions. In this year's auction, Kuldeep Sen, Vaibhav Arora, Kamlesh Nagarkoti, etc. are some of such names who had their base prices fixed at massive 20 lakhs rupees. There have been some famed players who failed to attract any franchise and were remained unsold. Some of them are Cheteshwar Pujara, Ajinkya Rahane, and others.

Readers, I have a point to make it here. Instead of spending a huge amount of money on overseas players, it will be wise enough to purchase only one or at the most two overseas players. This way we can save our foreign reserves and the saved money could be spent on purchasing more and more Indian talents.

A Tribute to the Legendary Shane Warne

The multifaceted Australian cricketer shocked the cricketing world with his untimely death on March 4. A calm and quiet Shane Warne will be remembered for his contributions in all three formats of the game. He was not only a fine leg-spin bowler having a precision of a surgeon in his deliveries, but he also made runs as well for his team. But the best came out from him in the 2008 edition of the IPL tournament when he captained a money ball team of Rajasthan Royals and sailed them to the coveted IPL cup. He was a superb coach and a versatile commentator in the later years of his career. Rajasthan Royals offered him mentorship in 2018. Playing for Team Australia, he broke many records in his career spanning over more than two decades. He was the first bowler to reach the 700 wickets mark in test matches in 2006 and held this record in his name till 2007. Interestingly he started his test career playing against India in 1992 in Sydney and had a special place in the hearts of Indians for his magical bowling spells and cool body language.

Shane Warne as a bowler: Lovingly called by nicknames "The Sheikh of Tweaks" and "The King", Shane Warne revolutionized the game of cricket by bringing back the dying art of leg-spin. He mastered over a difficult craft of delivering the leg breaks with his wrist in place of fingers and got his name entered in a rare specie of tweakers in the cricketing world. Any such bowler poses a difficult situation even for batters of the highest calibers. Examples are Sachin Tendulkar, Brian Lara, Nathan Astle, and likes who faced uneasiness in playing the maestro. With his mesmerizing deliveries, he picked up 708 wickets in test matches and 293 wickets in ODI's. 20 – 20 format was completely a new format during his times, despite that, he claimed 70 wickets in the shorter version of the game. He has a record of having the highest number of wickets (96) in one calendar year. Two of his best bowling spells are – 8/71 against England and 7/56 against South Africa. In the words of all-time great Allan Border, "Shane Warne is the Bradman of the leg-spin bowling".

Shane Warne as a captain and a coach: After the successful captaincy of English county Hampshire in 2007, he was appointed captain and coach of the IPL team Rajasthan Royals in 2008. He was a shrewd captain and understood every opponent batter and accordingly set the field and hand over the ball to the fittest bowler for that matter. In one of the matches against Deccan Chargers, he got rid of dangerous Adam Gilchrist by handing over the new ball to part-time off-spinner Yusuf Pathan in the power-play itself. Although he stunned everyone for his decision it paid and Gilchrist was back to Pavillion. He was never a silent captain and used to talk and brief his teammates continuously. He changed his plans according to the flow of the game.

Another example of his splendid captaincy was seen during the first edition of the IPL tournament 2008. His experience of leading Hampshire in domestic T-20 matches just before the IPL season gave him an edge over other fellow captains who did not have much knowledge of the new version of the game which has started only in 2007. His team Rajasthan Royals was written off by the sports lovers and fans who predicted that RR would finish in the bottom – half of the tournament. But it was his astute captaincy that even after losing three games at the league stage, the team bounced back and dared to defeat Delhi Daredevils and Chennai Super Kings, the teams which were full of star Indian and overseas players. It was his captaincy and coaching skills that an underdog team mostly with uncapped youngsters could win the final of 2008 IPL by 03 wickets. RR had won 13 out of the 16 games they had played and in the prize distribution ceremony, it was Shane Warne's Royals all the way.

Our tribute to legendary Shane Warne – the Wisden Cricketer of the century.

Despondency in Indian Women's Cricket

The twelfth edition of the ICC Women's Cricket World Cup 2022 has been scheduled in New Zealand from March 04 to April 03, 2022. The participating eight teams include Australia, England, New Zealand, South Africa apart from India, Pakistan, West Indies, and Bangladesh. The first four teams are known to be champions of the game of cricket. India is an emerging force in women's cricket while the remaining three are comparatively weak teams in women's cricket. Despite a fairly good kick-off in the tournament, Team India is back home even before the commencement of the semi-finals. Four teams that raced ahead of Team India are – Australia, England, South Africa, and West Indies. South Africa's victory against Team India on the last ball of their match despite Team India putting up a total of 274/7 gives enough reasons to analyze Team India's performance.

In the league stage, India's performance was lukewarm. India gave crushing defeats to teams – Pakistan, West Indies, and Bangladesh by more than 100 runs and lost fighting mighty Team Australia in the last 50th over even after piling up a total of 277/7. However, India received humiliating defeats against teams – New Zealand and England.

The Crucial Match Between India and South Africa: – After defeating three teams and getting defeated by three teams, India's entry to the semi-final was hanging on the result of the India vs South Africa match. A win in this match meant a semi-final ticket to Team India while the defeat meant India's immature exit from the tournament. India put up a handsome total of 274/7 for World Number 2 South Africa to chase. From India's side, Shafali Verma showed her worth by smashing 53 runs off 46 balls and Smriti Mandhana and Mithali Raj put up a brave show by scoring a partnership of 80 runs off 93 balls, both scoring their half-centuries. Harmanpreet Kaur also piled up a good score of 48 runs to provide India with its final total. India's fielding started with accurate bowling of Deepti Sharma, Rajeshwari Gayakwad, and Sneh Rana but due to lack of sharpness and variations and sting in their bowling apart from sloppy fielding, few unwanted overthrows and dropped catches could not stop South African batters from reaching near the fancy Indian total of 274. In the last over of the match, South Africa needed 7 runs in 6 balls. In the battle of nerves, South African batter Mignon du Preez dissipated the hope of Team India's entry in the semi-final when she hit the required 1 run on the last ball. This finalist of the T 20 2020 World Cup and ODI 2017 World Cup, the dejected Team India could not go beyond the league stage of the tournament.

The reported infighting between the team members, sub-standard bowling, fielding, and the injury of India's star captain Mithali

Raj all got piled up for India's early exit from the ICC Women's Cricket World Cup 2022.

It is hoped that BCCI will take note of these reasons and appoint a good head coach, preferably a lady cricketer. The possible commencement of women's s six-team IPL from 2023 will strengthen the women's cricket team with new talents.

Mumtaz Khan: From the Daughter of the Vegetable Vendor to the Daughter of India

Along a narrow dirty street at Topkhana Bazaar in Lucknow (UP) there lived parents of five daughters. Mother Qaiser Jahan and father Hafeez used to look after their family from the income they earned by selling vegetables from a vegetable cart. One of the daughters, Mumtaz Khan was passionate about running and playing hockey since childhood. Her mother was dead against her daughter wasting her time running and playing hockey as she wanted her to help them at their vegetable shop.

She was also not happy that her girl child should play a game meant for boys. Mumtaz found her way out by practicing only in her school and helping her parents after school hours to carry on with her passion. Her hockey journey began accidentally in 2011 when some selected students including Mumtaz were sent to take part in an athletics competition in Agra. Mumtaz ran her heart out and topped in the running events. Impressed by her deer-like speeds and energy level, the coach Neelam Siddique decided to groom her in the skills of hockey as speed and energy are the two important ingredients to excel in the game of hockey. She, therefore, decided to get Mumtaz admitted to KD Singh Babu Stadium in Lucknow. With her hard – work and dedication, she impressed all the coaches and was selected for a fellowship program. Under the guidance of expert coaches in hockey, she acquired mastery over dribbling the ball and giving and taking small passes. Her career with the Indian team in Under – 18 Asian Cup got a boost when India won the – Bronze and then in the Under – 18 Youth – Olympics India won the – Silver medal. Playing in the – Forward position her goals made India achieve these two big successes. But her best was yet to come. Having played more than 40 matches at the international level she was selected for the Indian junior hockey team as a center forward. The Indian team took part in the 2022 FIH Women's hockey junior World Cup held in South Africa from April 1 to April 12. Readers, let us have a look over the matches played at this prestigious tournament.

WOMEN'S HOCKEY JUNIOR WORLD CUP – In the biennial tournament, a total of 16 teams qualified for the final leg of the tournament. India was in the Pool – D along with Germany, Wales, and Malaysia. India topped its pool with 09 points, followed by Germany with 06 points. Both of them qualified for the quarter-finals. In the quarter-final, India beat South Korea by 3 – 0, with the first goal scored by Mumtaz. Mumtaz was also adjudged the – "Player Of The Match". India could not enter the final, as the

Dutch beat India by 3 – 0 in the first semi-finals. For the third and fourth positions, India clashed with England. The match got tied with a score of 2 – 2. For India, Mumtaz scored both the goals. The match was decided by the penalty – shootouts, in which India lost by 0 – 3. It was strange that Mumtaz was not given to hit any one of the three penalty shots and India had to satisfy at the Number 4.

Mumtaz was only the third top-scorer with a total of 08 goals in her kitty after the two players from The Netherlands with 13 and 11 goals.

It is rightly said that – "The winners never quit and the quitters never win" (Vince Lombardi), and if one dreams big there are people to help out. Thus a girl from a BPL family has proven to her parents that every cloud has a silver lining. For India, a new sensation in women's hockey has been born.

IPL – 2022

As with every good thing, IPL – 2022 also came to an end on May 29. This year's IPL will be in the minds of sports – lovers because of several reasons. Some of them are as follows: –

It was held only across four venues – three in Mumbai and one in Pune as against eight in the previous years. Out of the last four thrilling clashes, two were played in the iconic Eden Gardens of Kolkata, and the rest of the two including the final was played in the newly-built sprawling Narendra Modi cricket stadium in Ahmedabad. This stadium has a seating capacity of more than 1.30 lakhs spectators and has surpassed the Melbourne Cricket Ground with its capacity of 90,000. This is the largest cricket ground in the world.

Mumbai Indians's dashing batter Ishan Kishan was the most expensive buy of the year. It was bought for ₹. 15.25 crores. The most expensive overseas player was the Britisher Liam Livingstone who was bought by the Punjab Kings for ₹. 11.50 crores to play for them in the IPL.

A total of ten teams participated in the tournament including the two debutant teams – Gujarat Titans (GT) and Lucknow Super Giants (LSG). They have impressed with their superb cricketing skills while some of the powerhouse teams kept on struggling in the tournament. Out of the total 14 matches GT played, they won 10 and lost only 04 with a Net Run Rate (NRR) of + 0. 316 and ranked Number – 1 in the points table. The second newbie LSG won 09 matches from their 14 and was ranked at number three in the points table with an NRR of 0. 251. The team Rajasthan Royals (RR) sneaked between them with the second rank based on better its NRR than LSG.

This year's format was different than the previous years. Since several teams were, all the 10 teams were divided into two groups – Groups A and B, each having five teams. Round robin format was used till the last year.

Five-time IPL champions with star-studded players, Mumbai Indians led by national team captain Rohit Sharma stood last in the rankings due to their overconfidence and casual approach.

Rohit Sharma had his worst IPL season with a score of just 268 runs in 14 games and without a single half-century. Another disappointment came from all-time great smasher Virat Kohli who scored only 341 runs including three golden ducks. Team India's s famed speedster Jasprit Bumrah could claim only 15 wickets from 14 games, without claiming any wickets in half of the games he played. Other shocking performances came from Rishabh Pant (340 runs in 14 games), Venkatesh Iyer (182 runs in 12 games), and Team India's hope in its bowling attack Varun Chakravarthy (only 06 wickets in 11 games). The poor forms of the above players should be a cause of concern for the think-tank of Team

India as the T-20 I World Cup is scheduled in October this year.

BCCI for the first time awarded hefty incentives (₹. 1.25 crores) to the IPL curators and groundsmen.

This year's closing ceremony was quite impressive and glittering in which Bollywood star Ranveer Singh and Oscar-winning music maestro A. R. Rahman mesmerized the house packed with cricket lovers.

Out of 12 awards, half of them were taken away by the Britisher Jos Buttler of RR. These awards were given to felicitate the greatness of awardees.

Earlier, the players used to come from some select regions such as Mumbai, Delhi, Karnataka, Tamil Nadu, and up to a certain extent Gujarat and Punjab. But this year players came from even remote places of the country such as Nagaur, Moga, Chhindwara, Barmer, and others.

THE FINAL:– Gujarat Titans (GT), one of the two new franchises of this season, topped the league phase and entered the final played at their home – ground against the Rajasthan Royals (RR). GT aimed to win the final in their debut season, while RR had to take revenge for their thrashing defeat by GT in the first Qualifier match. GT's s sharp bowling attack led by its captain Hardik Pandya (3/17) restricted the formidable RR to a meager score of 130/9 after RR elected to bat. Pandya led his team from the front with both – bat and ball and guided his team with the contribution and consistency of each player and lifted the coveted IPL Cup 2022 by defeating RR by seven wickets. The superb leadership quality shown by Hardik Pandya in the ten-team league made him a national hero. Most of the cricket greats are of the view that the reign of Team India is handed over to young Pandya.

NEW FINDS:– This year's IPL has given so many exciting talents to choose from for the playing squad of Team India. The list is long. Some of the promising players who emerged from this IPL are as under:–

BATTERS:– Shivam Dube and Ruturaj Gaekwad (both from CSK), Rinku Singh (KKR), Deepak Hooda (LSG), Tilak Varma (MI, Yashasvi Jaiswal (RR), and Rajat Patidar (RCB).

BOWLERS:– Mukesh Choudhary (CSK), Mohsin Khan, Ravi Bishnoi, and Avesh Khan (all from LSG), Arshdeep Singh (PBKS), Kuldeep Sen and Prasidh Krishna (both from RR).

The Coming T-20 World Cup

This October will start the prestigious T 20 I World Cup in Australia. Each participating country prepares hard to make its claim for the cup. Team India is no different. The only occasion on which team India has won the cup was in 2007 under the leadership of MS Dhoni. BCCI has also planned to put up a winning show by scheduling important series against mighty England and West Indies to expose a young brigade of team India members under overseas conditions. These tours will be an audition of team India players for the World Cup.

In the process, team India recently had a 5 match T 20 I home – series against South Africa, played at New Delhi, Cuttack, Vishakhapatnam, Rajkot, and Bengaluru.

India managed to level the series after being 0 – 2 down. The fifth clash between the two became the decider as India dropped the series by winning the third and fourth matches. The much-awaited final scheduled at Bengaluru on June 19th was to be called off after rains played the spoilsport. Perhaps BCCI selected Bengaluru without doing any homework as it is a well-known fact that the monsoon remains active over the coastal areas during the third week of June.

India played the series under the leadership of its accidental captain Rishabh Pant following the injury of KL Rahul who was named as the captain in absence of national captain Rohit (Hitman) Sharma. Other key players who absented themselves were Virat Kohli, Jasprit Bumrah, Md. Shami, R. Ashwin, and R. Jadeja. On the other hand, Proteas had all the crucial players in the squad. The first game out of the five played at Arun Jaitley stadium in New Delhi was significant for team India as before this game they had registered 12 consecutive wins in T 20 I and they had a golden chance to create a world record of winning 13 games at a stretch in this format. But this did not happen to owe to the apathy of BCCI who let off star players remain absent from doing national duty in spite that the highest cricket body knew that India has won just one of their four T 20 I games against South Africa in India.

During the series, several grey areas in team India were observed. Although Pant is not a regular captain his captaincy was not an exceptional one and his similar pattern of dismissals in all the four matches puts a question mark on his inclusion in team India as a batter. His obesity, indecisiveness in selecting the batting orders, and inability to stay cool in difficult situations all came under the scanner.

India had a fragile opening combination in the form of Kishan and Gaekwad. Kishan has a minimal range of strokes and one should not be overwhelmed when occasionally he scores well too with the help of dropped catches. Moreover during the World Cup in Australia, extra pace and bounce on Australian pitches are bound to trouble this youngster who is not so – experienced on overseas wickets. The second opener, Gaekwad (96 runs in 05 games) was looking completely out of place especially to play on international wickets due to his current faulty technique against quality speedsters. He fell prey to rising and outgoing express deliveries of Proteas bowlers. The same thing can be said for Shreyas Iyer who repeatedly came at one down in the series despite his helplessness against quality speedsters. It was the sole efforts of middle-order batters, Hardik Pandya and fire-brand Karthik from sailing India out of a humiliating series defeat.

The bowling department also looked lame in absence of senior bowlers like Md. Shami and Bumrah. B. Kumar could swing the new ball and Avesh Khan's s physical power to bowl full-length bouncers which contained the Proteas smashers Miller, Dussen, Klaasen, and the captain Bavuma. These two should be the favorite choice of selectors out of the five pacers who could be in the World Cup playing squad. The spin department was handled by newcomer Axar Patel and Yuzvendra Chahal but both were indeed below par.

The above observations made based on the recently concluded India – South Africa T-20 I series indicate that selectors need to get a carefully selected mix of those senior and young players who could play well on overseas pitches which are notorious for their dangerous pace and uneven bounce.

India and England ODI Series

In the recent tour of England, India played one – held test match of the test – series of which four tests were played last September, three T 20 Is and three ODIs. In these matches, team India, comprising mostly of young cricketers, showed excellent cricketing skills with bat and ball resulting in the clinching of both the series of the shorter version of the game. The test series in which India was leading 2 – 1 ended in a 2 – 2 draw with the first test ending without a result after more than two days of play getting washed out.

T 20 I SERIES:–

The three-match T 20 I series was dominated by the young cricketers of India in every department of the game. The first two matches of the series were won by Team India which resulted in a lead of 2 – 0. The first T 20 match was memorable for both the captains – Rohit Sharma and Jos Buttler. Buttler lost his first match as a T 20 I captain of England who individually got out for a golden duck. For Rohit Sharma, it was the hitman's thirteenth consecutive win as a T 20 I captain. India took advantage of leading by 2 – 0 in the series and fielded all new cap speedsters for the third T 20 including Jammu express Umran Malik and newbie Arshdeep Singh. This was a good move to give youngsters exposure to playing on an overseas pitch. All the young speedsters played their hearts out for the team and restricted the star-studded English team's victory just by 17 runs and the series ended with 2 – 1.

ODI SERIES: -

With the T 20 I World Cup getting closer, the two series were seen as a trial for the players. Although India won this series by 2 – 1 despite star players Sharma and Kohli struggling to find their forms, it is necessary to examine the performance of each player in the light of the coming World Cup.

PERFORMANCE OF BATTERS: -

Captain Rohit Sharma had an excellent start to the ODI series with 76* from 58 balls paving way for an emphatic victory by ten wickets and acknowledging the efforts of the bowlers who wrapped up the English innings for merely 110 runs. But, the hitman failed miserably in the remaining two matches of the series finishing with just 93 runs in the entire series. The blue-eyed boy of cricket lovers Virat Kohli disappointed like on many other occasions and scored 16 and 17 in the two matches that he got to bat. Perhaps, he is paying for his habit of edging outswingers as on both occasions he succumbed to England's express left-arm pacers Willey and Topley. The performance of these two stars of Indian cricket is indeed a cause of concern for the selectors and sports – lovers alike. The third ODI will be remembered for the grand show by wicketkeeper-batter Rishabh Pant who slammed his maiden ODI century of 125* hitting ruthlessly 16 boundaries and 02 sixes on the bowling of all English pacers all along the ground. Particularly he was merciless towards his bowling of Willey and hit five consecutive fours in one over. It was amazing to see Pant desisting his in-built attacking instinct and batting so cautiously to build – up his inning of 125*. He also showed good keeping skills and took five catches behind the stumps in the series. India's new hero in the shorter version of the game is none other than Hardik Pandya. He has repeatedly proved himself an important player for team India in the two shorter formats of the game. His heroics in the game started with winning the IPL – 2022 for the Gujarat Titans (GT) and since then he has not disappointed cricket lovers. His spell of 4/24 in 07 overs coupled with quickfire 71 runs from 55 balls helped team India to win the ODI series. Making 100 runs in the series and taking 06 wickets with an average of 4. 35 speak of his excellent form with bat and ball before the World Cup. Disappointments came from Shikhar Dhawan, Suryakumar Yadav (SKY), and R. Jadeja. Dhawan, an experienced and dependable opener for India in no way proved himself to be in the squad of team India for the World Cup. In ODIs – 2 and 3, he fell prey to the quality pacer Topley finding himself uncomfortable against the speedster and could score only 10 runs. In ODI – 1, he used 54 balls of the powerplay to make only 31. Suryakumar Yadav got to play only two innings and scored only 43 runs in the two games. An impressive hitter of the white ball, SKY was far behind for which he is known. The second all-rounder of the team, Ravindra Jadeja struggled throughout the series with his form and could claim only one wicket in nine overs in the two games that he got to play.

PERFORMANCE OF BOWLERS: –

India played with its four pacers: – Bumrah, Md. Shami, two newcomers – Md. Siraj and Prasidh Krishna. With his quality outswingers and superb Yorkers coupled with a speed of 135 and more, Bumrah is bound to be the most dangerous bowler on overseas pitches. Team India has high hopes for him in the upcoming World Cup. In this ODI series, he became the highest wicket-taker for India with eight wickets at an economy rate of 3.92. He bowled his career – best of 6/19 in the first ODI and was responsible for sending the top batting order of England resulting in England's total score of 110. Another match-winner for India, Md. Shami put up an excellent show with the ball although he could claim only four wickets in the three matches at an economy – the rate of 4. 87. With his pace, he troubled hard-hitters of white – ball namely, Buttler and Livingstone. The third pacer, Prasidh Krishna needs to get much more exposure on foreign pitches before he could be picked up for important games. In the entire ODI series of three matches, he got only two wickets off 22 overs with a high economy – the rate of 5.77. In absence of Bumrah in the third ODI, Md. Siraj got a chance in the team but could not show his worth after giving away many runs to finish with 2/66 in 09 overs, which he bowled. However, he claimed Joe Root and Bairstow, the two dangerous players of the England team which shows his potential. The spin department was in the hands of spanky Yuzvendra Chahal and all-rounder Ravindra Jadeja. Chahal showed his prominence in the team when he destroyed the top-order of England, comprising Bairstow, Root, and Stokes in ODI – 2 and finished with 4/47. In the third ODI, he claimed three wickets, although he gave away 60 runs.

Thus, the young brigade of team India has lots of potential and must be the reason for team India to give a brave show in the World Cup against mighty Australia, Kiwis, and Britishers.

BCCI Sponsored Merry making Tours for Indian Cricket Team

The prestigious T-20 I Cricket World Cup is scheduled to commence on October 16th, 2022. Winning a World Cup irrespective of its format is the dream of every cricket-playing team and the players of each team sweat them out in intensive preparedness. Contrary to it, BCCI kept its senior players like captain Rohit Sharma, Virat Kohli, Rishabh Pant, Jasprit Bumrah, Md. Shami and others are away from practice sessions in the name of giving them – 'rest'. Moreover, it programmed three tours for Team India for fun and frolic to play cricket with teams of Ireland, West Indies (including two in the USA), and Zimbabwe between June and August ignoring the fact facts that the World Cup is hardly six-seven weeks away. It will not be out of place to mention here that these three teams are having very low ICC Rankings. These tours could have been organized after the World Cup and the time thus saved should have been properly utilized in giving the players intensive and rigorous coaching, especially the younger lot, who are likely to get selected for the team in the World Cup. But, it seems that the BCCI has learned no lesson from the previous World Cup – 2021 when Pakistani speedster Shaheen Afridi created havoc and became the reason for Team India's exit at the league stage itself. Let us hope that history does not repeat itself in this World Cup.

Readers, to give you a brief account of the above tours a quick review of the matches is being given here :

1. IRELAND TOUR (IRELAND'S T 20 I RANKING IS 12):– In this tour, Team India was led by Hardik Pandya in absence of Rahul and Sharma, and the team played two T-20 I matches. In both the matches, Team India won by 07 wickets and 04 runs

respectively. Although Team Ireland is in a learning stage, it put Team India in the hot water for its victory and India could win the second match merely by four runs despite Irish captain Balbirnie's heroic innings of 60 runs. Both the matches were played at The Village Cricket Stadium, Malahide, Ireland.

2. WEST INDIES TOUR (WEST INDIES T 20 I RANKINGS IS 07 AND ODI RANKINGS IS 09): – In this tour,

India was led by Shikhar Dhawan in the ODIs and Rohit Sharma in the T-20 Is. India played three ODIs and five T 20. India won the 03-match ODI series, 3 – 0. The Windies were led by Nicholas Pooran in both formats. In the first ODI, India won a thriller of a match by 03 runs, due to the efforts of skipper Shikhar Dhawan (97), Shubman Gill (64), and Shreyas Iyer (54).

In the second ODI, India defeated the Windies by 02 wickets. India chased down a massive total of 312 at the loss of 08 wickets with 02 balls to spare. Axar Patel (64*) is top-scored for India.

The third and final ODI was a rain-marred one. India posted 225/3 in 36 overs. In reply, the Windies were chasing the revised target of 257 runs in 35 overs but were bowled out for only 137 runs in 26 overs. India won the match by 119 runs (D/L method) and completed the whitewash in the series by 3 – 0.

In the five-match T-20 I series, out of which 03 matches took place in West Indies, and the other two in Florida, USA, India registered a 4 – 1 series win over the Windies. Rohit Sharma captained the Indian side, whereas Nicholas Pooran was leading the Windies side.

In the first T-20 I, India managed to get better off the Windies by 68 runs. India put up a total of 190/6 in the 20 overs, whereas the Windies managed only 122/8 in their 20 overs.

In the second T-20 I, the Windies defeated India by 05 wickets. In this match, India bowled out for 138 runs in 19. 4 overs, whereas the Windies chased the target (141/5 in 19. 2 overs). Obed Mc Coy of West Indies produced a career-best performance of 6/17 in his 04 overs, the best by any West Indian in the shorter formats of the game. This performance earned him the Man Of The Match award.

In the third T-20 I, India defeated the Windies by 07 wickets. West Indies made 164/5 in their allotted 20 overs. India chased down the target and reached 165/3 after playing 19 out of the 20 overs.

In the fourth T 20 I, India managed to score 191/5 in their allotted 20 overs. Chasing the target of 192, West Indies were bundled out for 132 in 19. 1 overs. India won the match by 59 runs, and also sealed the series, 3 – 1.

In the fifth and final T-20 I, held the very next day, after the fourth T-20 I was also won by India. India put up a huge total of 188/7 in their allotted 20 overs. Chasing the total, the Windies team was bowled out for a low score of 100 runs in 15. 4 overs. India won the match by 88 runs and sealed the series by a margin of 4 – 1.

The final two T-20 I matches were played in Florida, USA, whereas the first three T-20 I matches were played in the Caribbean Islands.

Rookie left-arm medium-pacer Arshdeep Singh of India for his superb bowling performances in the entire series was adjudged as the Man Of The Series.

3. ZIMBABWE TOUR (ZIMBABWE ODI RANKINGS IS 13): – In this three-match tour, India was led by

Shikhar Dhawan, whereas the newly-built Zimbabwean team was led by their newly appointed keeper-skipper, Regis Chakabva. In the first ODI, the Zimbabwean team scored 189/all out in 40. 3 overs. Chasing the target, India reached the target of 190 in 30. 5 overs. Openers Shikhar Dhawan and Shubman Gill reached the target without the loss of any wicket.

In the second ODI, Zimbabwe once again batted first and scored a total of 161 runs in 38. 1 overs. Chasing the target, India reached the target of 162 runs in 25. 4 overs. Sanju

Samson is top-scored for India with 43* runs. India won the match and the series, 2 – 0.

In the final and third ODI, for the first time in the series, India batted first and put up a huge total of 289/8 in the allotted 50 overs. Chasing down the target of 290, the Zimbabwean team displayed a superb performance, riding on the brilliant knock of Sikandar Raza, who scored a magnificent ton of 115 runs in 95 balls. India managed to win the match by 13 runs and completed a clean sweep of the series, 3 – 0. Shubman Gill was declared the Man Of The Match in the Final match, as well as The Man Of The Tournament.

All three matches were played at the Harare Sports Club Cricket Ground, Harare, Zimbabwe.

The Plight of Indian Men's Cricket Team

The agony of the Indian men's cricket team's ouster from the T 20 I World Cup – 2021 at the league stage itself is still fresh in the minds of cricket lovers. It seems neither BCCI nor our players have learned any lesson from this humiliating defeat. Once again, Team India is knocked out of the Asia Cup Tournament after getting defeated in two consecutive matches in Super – the 4 levels by the arch-rival (Pakistan) and ICC T-20 I 08th ranked -team Sri Lanka in the Super – 4 stages. Remarkably, only six teams participate in the Asia Cup, out of which the four teams namely – Hong Kong, Afghanistan, Bangladesh, and Sri Lanka have very poor ratings in the ICC T 20 I rankings. Hong Kong was not even given direct entry into the tournament. The question is how Team India will come out of the predicament.

The outcome of the Asia Cup for Team India becomes more gruesome given the upcoming T 20 I World Cup in October this year. It, therefore, becomes a compulsion to find out the reasons for Team India falling flat on its face.

 # Reasons for Team India's Miserable Performance: –

1. Faulty Selection of Playing – XI: – Till the last match, India was struggling to find a robust opening pair. The experimentation is still on. KL Rahul was asked to open the inning with Rohit Sharma. Rahul has no experience in making a perfect opening partner. This resulted in his inability to provide a good start with his inconsistent captain. The duo could make only one opening partnership of 50 runs or more. Every time Rahul failed and one down Virat Kohli practically, who himself is struggling with his form, opened the innings. Moreover, Rahul was not on the team for more than two months due to an injury. He made just 70 runs in the four

matches he played. Perhaps, BCCI and our team management go for the selection of playing – XI based on their likings or dislikings of a player. That is why they did not pick up Shubman Gill despite his excellent run – rate in the matches he played before the Asia Cup. Which international team is without its fixed opening partner? This is a puzzle that needs answers from the BCCI. It is now known that Suryakumar Yadav and Rishabh Pant have minimal cricketing shots for any lack in providing good runs at the number – 2 and number – 3 positions. Such underperforming players should not be retained together in the national team. In the two innings that Pant batted, he could make only 31 runs from 25 balls by playing as a three-down batter.

As far as the middle – order is concerned, which is the backbone of any team, team management got pleasure in experimenting with the idea of preferring Pant over Dinesh Karthik. Karthik did superbly well in the recently – concluded IPL and was found to be a useful finisher in IPL – 2022. Technically also Karthik is much experienced as a batter as well as a stumper. The decision of dropping Karthik from the playing – XI of the Asia Cup is a mystery. Another middle-order batter, Hardik Pandya also lost his golden touch in batting and could not give support to the sinking batting line-up of Team India.

Bowling Department: – In the tournament, Team India experimented with playing only with three seamers namely – Bhuvneshwar Kumar, Hardik Pandya, and the inexperienced newbie Arshdeep Singh. B. Kumar showed poor form in his bowling having very little pace to utilize the initial dew on the pitch while Pandya also failed with the ball. He gave away 44 runs to claim a single wicket in his quota of 04 overs in the match against Pakistan and went wicketless after giving away 35 runs against the all-important match with Sri Lanka. Hardik's technique of giving short balls and claiming the wickets by getting the batters caught did not work with the acclaimed players of Pakistan and Sri Lanka. His childish technique of claiming the wickets may be good for the IPL but certainly

may not work for the international players and batters of teams – Australia, New Zealand, and England in the upcoming World Cup. This is high time that India gets its fourth seamer groomed from amongst the super-express speedsters – Umran Malik, Avesh Khan, Mohsin Khan, and Md. Siraj. Keeping Shami out of the squad is certainly an injustice to the veteran Indian pacer. Will selectors come out with any explanations for his non-inclusion and making the bowling department a flop show in the entire Asia Cup? It was difficult for Team India to restrict the runs in the death overs.

Selectors seem to be very harsh on off-spinner Ravichandran Ashwin by dropping him quite often without any reason. They preferred two-leg – spinners instead of playing a combination of one leg and one off-spinner. Team India paid a heavy price against the match with Pakistan, when its leftie Mohammad Nawaz attacked harshly on the leg-spinners duo by smashing 42 runs over their bowling in just 20 balls. Selectors had made similar mistakes by preferring inexperienced Varun Chakravarthy over Ashwin in the previous World Cup – 2021. This superfluous mistake of selectors against New Zealand became the main reason for India's early ouster from the previous World Cup – 2021. Do Don t our selectors like the face of Ashwin?

(2). Rohit Sharma as a Captain: – There is no doubt that Sharma is a great opening batter that Team India has ever produced but when captaincy comes, the bulky hitman certainly lacks the power to taking quick decisions as to when to use change in bowling and batting orders. This gentleman captain lacks the shrewdness required by a captain. Therefore, the team – management and the selectors which include captains are not on the same page. As an example, he could never think of handing over the ball to part-time bowler Deepak Hooda. Moreover, Sharma has very less experience with the captaincy in international matches. It is hoped that he has learned a lesson from the humiliating ouster of Team India from the Asia Cup – 2022.

It is further hoped that our selectors will not give a deaf ear to the suggestions coming in from the experts and they will go for a properly balanced team in India for the upcoming World Cup – 2022. Otherwise, the situation will coincide with the popular Bollywood song – "Sab Kuch Luta ke hosh mein aaye to kya Hua".

Asia Cup 2022 and It's New Heroes

Asia Cup – 2022 got over on September 11 with the final match between Pakistan and Sri Lanka after its commencement getting postponed thrice – firstly in October 2020, secondly in June 2021, and then in October 2021. The reasons were – the spread of the pandemic from 2020 and then political unrest and economical crisis in Sri Lanka. Finally, it could start on August 27th and conclude on September 11th and was played on the two grounds of Sharjah and Dubai. A natural question arises in the minds of sports lovers why there is only the Asia Cup, although there are seven continents in the globe? The answer is simple. Asia is the only continent where there is a number of international cricketing teams needed to conduct a proper tournament.

This year in 2022 10 International cricketing teams was ready to participate. However, the tournament was held between six teams – five teams being ICC recognized test-sides, while Hong Kong from the remaining 04 teams got its entry based on coming on the top in the matches played amongst five non-test sides (called Qualifiers). The six teams were divided into two groups of three teams each, out of which the top two teams from both groups qualified for the final. Team India, although entered the Super – 4 but could not reach the final after losing two consecutive matches against Pakistan and Sri Lanka, and thus team India was shown the door.

Interestingly, team India has won the Asia Cup for the maximum number of times (7) out of 14 editions of the tournament followed by Sri Lanka (5 times) and Pakistan (2 times). 2012 Asia Cup was memorable for the Master Blaster Sachin Tendulkar as he reached the landmark of completing his 100th international century. That match was played with Bangladesh.

Before 2016, Asia Cup was being played in the ODI format of 50 overs. Then after, due to the lukewarm response of the sports lovers to watch the matches of 50 overs, ICC decided to host the Asia Cup in the T 20 format.

Most of us remain unaware of the magical talents possessed by upcoming players outside India in their cricketing skills. In this write-up, we will get to know the talents of players who excelled consistently in this year's Asia Cup.

NEW HEROES OF THE ASIA CUP: –

i. Bhanuka Rajapaksa: – The bulky-batter from Sri Lanka was instrumental in registering Sri Lanka's victory over Pakistan in the final. In that match, he smashed 71* runs in just 45 balls. More importantly, he came out to bat when Sri Lanka was reeling at 76 / 3 in the Powerplay itself. He architected Sri Lanka's win in the final by getting two partnerships of 58 runs and 44 runs with two Sri Lankan batters – Hasaranga and Karunaratne. For his superb batting talent in this match, he was awarded – "Player Of The Match". His performance was consistent throughout the tournament with an average of 38. 20 by amassing 191 runs in the total 06 matches that Sri Lanka played in the tournament.

ii. Pramod Madhushan: – The 28-year-old right-arm medium pacer Pramod debuted for Sri Lanka in the second last match of the Asia Cup. In the first match played against Pakistan in the Super – 4, he claimed the prize wicket of Md. Rizwan gave Pakistan a shock. He finished with the figures of 2/21 in 2. 2 overs but the miracle was yet to come from him. He broke the nerves of the Pakistan batting line-up when he claimed the versatile Pakistan skipper Babar Azam and it's another batter, Fakhar Zaman for ducks. He also claimed the important wickets of Iftikhar Ahmed (32) and Naseem Shah (04). He finished his deadly bowling – spell with figures of 4 – 0 – 34 – 4. His superb bowling spell became one of the reasons for Sri Lanka to lift the cup and Sri Lanka has high hopes for this medium-fast speedster.

iii. Wanindu Hasaranga: – One of the most feared leggies in the international cricket of current times, Hasaranga claimed 09 crucial wickets in all the 06 matches that Sri Lanka played in the Cup. In the final, he smashed 36 runs off 21 balls helping his side for putting up a total of 170/6. For his consistent performance throughout the tournament, he was awarded as the – "Player Of The Tournament".

iv. Pathum Nissanka: – The stylish 24 – year old Sri Lankan opener Nissanka piled up 173 runs with an average of 34. 60. A good smasher of the ball, he scored his half-century (52 runs off 37 balls) in the Super – 4 matches against Team India. His other half-century (55*) came in the Super – 4 match against Pakistan in just 48 deliveries against Pakistan's s superb bowling attack. This youngster will certainly be an important cricketer for Sri Lanka in the future.

v. Kusal Mendis: – Sri Lankan team experimented it's stumper – batter by promoting him to the opening slot from the middle – order. Kusal did – not disappoint the team – management and justified his promotion by scoring a total of 155 runs in the tournament. His 37 – balls 60 runs and 37 – balls 57 runs in the innings played respectively against Bangladesh and India helped his team in advancing in the tournament.

vi. Naseem Shah: – The 19 year baby of the Pakistan team is certainly a revolution in the pace – bowling arena. Debuting in the Group – stage match against India, he created panic in the Indian camp by dispatching KL Rahul and Suryakumar Yadav in the Powerplay itself. He picked up 7 wickets in the 5 matches that he played for Pakistan. The best came from him not as a bowler but as a batter when in the crucial match of Pakistan with Afghanistan he hit two consecutive sixes on the first two balls of the 20th over to seal a thrilling victory for his side and paved the way for

Pakistan to enter the final. It was these two sixes that shut the door for Team India to enter the final.

vii. Mohammad Nawaz: – He is known for his bowling skill, but he thrilled the cricket lovers with the bat as well. Seeing his hidden batting talent, he was promoted to the Number 4 position which he fully justified by hitting 42 runs off 20 balls and became the – "Player Of The Match" to beat Team India by 05 wickets.

viii. Shadab Khan: – This 23-year-old leggie became the Hero of the Tournament when he helped Pakistan to register a 155 – run victory. He claimed 4 wickets for Afghanistan by giving away just 8 runs in his spell of 2. 4 overs. In all, he picked up 8 wickets.

Apart from the above players, World Cricket has high hopes from Khushdil Shah (Pakistan) and Fazalhaq Farooqi (Afghanistan).

Australia - The New World Test Champion by Deepanshu Srivastava

The World Test Championship 2021-2023 Finale was held between India and Australia at the prestigious Oval ground of England from June 7 to June 11. The mighty Kangaroos beat team India ruthlessly by a whopping margin of 209 runs and became the second test team to win the Mace. Rohit Sharma led the Indian team displayed a shameful performance in all the 3 departments of the game. Team India's defeat was clearly due to the shocking surrender of its high-profile batters - Sharma, Kohli, Pujara, and Gill- against the quality bowling of Australia. The Oval Surface is known for its variable bounce and Aussie pacers mainly Scott Boland exploited the weakness of playing -going stump balls of Indian top order batters, mainly Kohli and Gill. Boland's rare quality of bowling spell in both innings by compelling the Indian batters to play outside the off stump deliveries shut the door to Indian hope of winning the Championship on the second consecutive occasion. India had lost to the Kiwis in the first edition of the game in 2021. As far as Indian bowlers are concerned, the pace duo of Md.Shami and Md. Siraj failed miserably to contain the run flow even from Aussies lower order batters.

The third pacer, Umesh Yadav also could not impress with the red ball.

REASONS FOR THE DISMAL PERFORMANCE OF TEAM INDIA

The following are the main reasons for Team India's humiliating defeat :

1. Unmindful team selection-

The exclusion of ICC test no.1 rank bowler R. Ashwin from playing 11 was the most disastrous decision.

Right-handed spinner Ashwin would have been the match-winner for the Indian team as the Aussies team had 3 left-hand batters in their playing 11. The cricket legend Tendulkar, in a press statement, has expressed his displeasure over Ashwin's exclusion. The inclusion of yester-year pacer Umesh Yadav puts a question mark on the wisdom of the selection committee. He was proved to be a liability for team India.

2. BCCI is, perhaps, the only board amongst the world cricketing boards which has had no chief selector for almost 4 years! How, then, is team India selected? Has BCCI become 1- man board?

3. Our legendary cricketers like Tendulkar, Gavaskar, Shastri, and their likes also don't want to take responsibility for selecting the best playing 11 for ICC tournaments by taking over the reins of the selection committee once the post is advertised. Perhaps they prefer to comment on the selection through the media after the team is defeated.

HISTORY OF THE WORLD TEST CHAMPIONSHIP

ICC World Test Championship (WTC) is a league tournament for test cricket. In October 2017, the league was planned to involve the top 9 test teams. Through a Point Percentage system, the top two teams amongst 9 teams, after playing test series over 2 years, qualify for the WTC Final. Team India entered into the Final of the 2021-2023 edition after playing 18 test series, out of which they won 10 series and lost 5. Three test series were drawn. India was also in the final during its first edition, 2019 -2021, but at that time also Rohit Sharma led the team got convincingly defeated by the Kiwis.

It is hoped that team India will come out as a winner in the 2023 - 2025 edition of the Championship as the team India is full of talent and has the potential to win. The only prerequisite is the proper team selection through a selection committee comprising legendary cricketers.

Indian Premier League - 2023: A New Beginning By Deepanshu Srivastava

One of the biggest sports carnivals in the country, the IPL, is underway since March 31, 2023, in its new avatar. The 16th season of IPL which is a franchise 20-20 Cricket league in India, organized by the BCCI, has now returned to its original home and away home format after 4 long years since 2019 due to the pandemic. The previous 3 seasons - 2020 to 2022 - got sacrificed due to Covid -19 and were held at neutral venues leaving Sports lovers in India deprived of the yearly event loved and waited by all age groups.

A group stage 20-20 format tournament, having 10 teams, is divided into 2 groups of

5 teams where all of them put their hearts out to clinch the coveted IPL trophy. The the tournament is spread over 70 league-stage matches and 4 playoffs.

As on May 13, 59 league matches have been played and the race for reaching the Playoffs is at its peak with the current 16th season heading towards its final phase, making the cricket lovers hold their breaths in search of the king of IPL 2023.

In its new avatar, several changes have been made by the BCCI, the prominent of all being the provision of IMPACT PLAYER and the DRS for no balls and wide balls. Apart from it, the two teams have to submit the list of their playing 11 AFTER the toss.

IMPACT PLAYER RULE -This is a major change in the 15 years history of IPL. According to the rule, a team has to declare 5 additional players apart from the playing 11, and any one player from the playing squad can be substituted from the 5 other players during the ongoing inning of the team. Such a player is called the Impact Player. With the introduction of this rule, now setting or chasing a target of 200 or more runs seems to have become easier. The audience is now getting more time to enjoy the thrill of the game.

ADDITIONAL DRS Apart from the usual DRS, directly the captains can appeal for a review of the umpire's call on a no-ball or a wide delivery. This change in rules has brought surgical precision to the game.

RE-INTRODUCTION OF FAN PARKS

The ongoing 16th edition of IPL brings back the IPL Fan Parks after 2019. A large open space is made available away from the match venue on the weekends where sports lovers can watch and feel the match live on large TV screens amidst quality family time while enjoying the Kids Zone and Food park facilities. The Fan Parks, this time, is spread over 45 cities. On the day of the IPL final on May 28th, the Fan Parks will be in 5 cities including Jammu and Jorhat.

OTHER HIGHLIGHTS

1. The new young sensation, Arshdeep Singh did an unbelievable when he broke the middle stumps in his 2 consecutive deliveries in an over and sent two Mumbai Indians batters back to the dug-outs. The breaking of stumps has cost BCCI approximately 24 lakhs, and one wicket fitted with LED bulbs costs around 12 lakhs INR. The incident should wake up the IPL Committee to scrutinize the quality control of the kits supplied.

2. The RCB players wore green jerseys in Bengaluru Stadium playing against team RR to showcase their commitment towards green. The finest part of this Go Green innovative idea is that the jerseys are made of recycled waste materials collected at the stadium. Reportedly 8 tonnes of recyclable waste materials are generated after every match. This innovative idea has made team RCB the World's first Carbon neutral Cricket team.

3. The 42nd clash between the teams of RR and MI was the 1000th match played in IPL till then.

4. The present form of Virat Kohli may not be good but still, he is the most loved cricketer in the audience. Kohli became the FIRST batter to complete 7000 IPL runs at Arun Jaitley Stadium, New Delhi on May 6 playing for his franchise RCB against the team DC. On the occasion, a pavilion in the Stadium was also named after him.

5. On May 7 during the match between the teams of GT and LSG, Hardik Pandya and Krunal Pandya became the FIRST brothers to captain their teams and that match became Pandya vs Pandya match.

POSSIBLE TEAMS FOR PLAYOFFS

The current top 5 teams as on May 10 in the 10-team IPL points table are the teams GT, CSK, MI, LSG, and RR. Although it is most challenging to shortlist the first 4 teams, seeing the closed contest going on, closely observing their team compositions and their previous match performances, it seems that out of the above 5 teams, 4 will make their way to the Play-Offs.

KAUN BANEGA IPL 2023 KING

The million dollar question haunting the sports lovers pan India is the name of IPL -2023 Champion.

The best two teams as of now are certainly the teams of GT and CSK and the winner will be the team that outsmarts the other in all the 3 departments of the game. The mind game between the two captains - Hardik and MSD- will also play a crucial role in the outcome of the match and both the captains are known to be top game changers through their mind games. Let us keep our fingers crossed till the late evening of the final day, May 28.

Footballers of the World-1: FIFA World Cup 2022

It is an excellent opportunity to watch in action the world-class footballers and their soccer skills through the ongoing FIFA (Federation Internationale De Football Association) World Cup. FIFA is held every after 4 years. Its inaugural edition was held way back in 1930. Its format is composed of the qualification phase to determine the main stage of the tournament participated by 32 nations (round of 64). Since 1930, Brazil has won the tournament for a maximum of 8 times. FIFA 2022 is currently being held in Qatar, UAE from November 20, and the final clash will be held on December 18. All 32 participating nations are divided into 8 groups, Group A to Group H. Readers, in this series, we will bring the highlights of the matches being played in Qatar.

HIGHLIGHTS OF THE MATCHES PLAYED BETWEEN November 20 to 24:

1. Match No 1

   The inaugural match was played between host Qatar and Ecuador (Ecuador is a tiny country in South America, Spanish being its official language). In this match Ecuador came out victorious, defeating Qatar by 2-0). It was only the second match of Qatar in the World Cup.

2. Match No 2

   It was played between England and Iran. England comfortably won the match by a margin of 6-2.

3. Match No 3

   Senegal and Holland clashed in this match (Senegal is a West African nation that has the distinction of defeating a great name in football, France in the 2006 edition of the WC). This match was won by Holland 2-0

4. Match No 4

   It was played between the USA and New South Wales (NSW came into existence in 2021 after the famous Brexit). The match was tied with a score of 1-1. NSW held team US, a veteran, playing skillfully.

5. Match No 5

   Saudi Arabia and mighty Argentina locked horns in the match, in which SA stunned the soccer-loving audience by defeating Argentina by 2-1 despite the presence of one of the great footballers of the century, Messi.

6. Match No 6

   Played between Denmark and Tunisia, a country in North Africa, it went goalless from either side with a score of 0-0

7. Match No 7

   Mexico City and Polland played this match another match which went goalless.

8. Match No 8

   The two teams, France and Australia, both known to be world-class teams displayed excellent skills in the game in which France thrashed Australia by 4-1.

9. Match No 9

   Played between Morocco and Croatia (located at the crossroad of Central and SE Europe), both lesser known in the game, also went 0-0.

10. Match No 10

    One of the greats in World Soccer, Germany clashed with Japan, and it was surprisingly won by Japan by 2-1, although Germany was leading by 1-0 till 75 the minute of the game. Japan came back into the game strongly and managed two goals in the last phase of the game.

11. Match No 11

    Spain and Costa Rica, a country of Central America, was dominated by mighty Spain and the one-sided game was won by it by 7-0.

12. Match No 12

Canada and Belgium played this encounter and it was won by Belgium, a contender in this year's Cup, by 1-0

13. Match No 13

Switzerland and Cameroon, a country in Central Africa, played the match and it was won by Switzerland by 1-0.

14. Match No 14

The match between Uruguay and South Korea went goalless, although Uruguay was the favorite of soccer lovers of the game.

15. Match No 15

Portugal and Ghana played the match in which Portugal defeated Ghana by 3-2. Ronaldo from Portugal, a household name in the world of football, scored one goal.

Footballers of the World–2: FIFA World Cup 2022

In this part of the article, we have described the highlights of the matches being played in Qatar from Nov 25 to November 28 as part of the FIFA World Cup 2022 (Match No 16 to 30).

During this period, defending champion France of group D and Holland of group A almost confirmed their places in pre – quarter-final. The host Qatar got the distinction of getting out of the race of entering into the pre -QF after losing both of its matches during this period. Subsequently, their journey in the world cup came to an end. Other countries whose claims in this world cup ended are Serbia and Canada. Other possible contenders of the Cup, such as Belgium, Germany, Argentina, and Brazil made their positions strong in their respective matches.

Let us know about the matches played in this part of the game.

16. Match No 16

In the one-sided match played between Brazil and Serbia, Brazil comfortably defeated Serbia by 2-0.

17. Match No 17

New South Wales and Iran clashed in the match and to anybody's guess, Iran defeated NSW by 2-0. Both goals were field goals.

18. Match No 18

Host Qatar took on Senegal and the match was won by Senegal by the score of 3-1.

This was Qatar's first and only goal scored in the world cup.

19. Match No 19

Played between one of the title contenders Holland and Ecuador and the result surprised many when Ecuador held Holland for a 1-1 draw.

20. Match No 20

England and USA locked horns in the match which went goalless. The field plan of the US made England, the better of the two teams, helpless and the result was a draw.

21. Match No 21

In the group D encounter between Australia and Tunisia, Australia managed to get better off Tunisia by a slender margin of 1-0.

22. Match No 22

Poland and Saudi Arabia match was won by Poland by 2-0, although SA had created the first major upset of this tournament by defeating the strong team Argentina by 2-1.

23. Match No 23

Played between the title holder France and Denmark, France as expected defeated Denmark comfortably by the margin of 2-1. It is interesting to note that a team like France was trailing behind by 1-0 till the first half of the game.

24. Match No 24

The notable match between two good teams in the tournament – Argentina and Mexico – was won by Argentina by 2-0. It was Argentina's first victory in spite of the presence of all-time great Messi in the team.

25. Match No 25

Japan and Costa Rica played the match and to utter surprise, Japan which had done the second major upset of the tournament when they had defeated Germany could not do any wonders and got defeated 1-0.

26. Match No 26

Played between Belgium and Morocco, this group F match was won by Morocco by 2-0 leaving the soccer-loving people stunned. The result of this match was one of the biggest upsets so far. The two goals scored by Morocco were done in the additional time.

27. Match No 27

Croatia and Canada played the match in which Canada was crushed by a margin of 4-1. Croatia proved its supremacy in both parts of the game and showed its intention to move ahead in style.

28. Match No 28

One of the much-awaited matches between Spain and Germany got tied by 1-1. The sports lovers enjoyed the match and saw the two greats of Football trying to bring a result. In the match, Spain was ahead till the 83rd minute of the match.

29. Match No 29

    Cameroon and Serbia clashed in this group G match, which was another drawn match. The score was 3-3. Cameroon was trailing in the entire first half but strongly came back in the match in the last few minutes of the game. However, both teams had upset their opponents earlier in this tournament.

30. Match No 30

    Between South Korea and Ghana, the two bottom-placed teams in the tournament, the match was edged out in favor of Ghana by 3-2.

Footballers of the World–3: FIFA World Cup 2022

After the highlights of the first 30 matches of FIFA World Cup 2022 being played in Qatar in the first two parts of this series of articles, we now present to you the highlights of another 15 matches (match no. 31 to 45) which were played between November 28 and December 2. The total matches which will be played are 64 in the prestigious World Cup. The 31st match was played between Brazil and Switzerland and the 45th match, was between South Korea and Portugal. During this period 16 teams got themselves entered into the pre-quarter-final (round of 16), ousting the remaining 16 teams from the world cup. Those teams which entered the pre – QF stage comprised of some surprising entries, almost unexpectedly such as Japan, and Morocco. It was almost a heartbreak for Belgium, the World no2 team according to the FIFA WORLD ranking, and for World no 11, one-time World Cup holder, Germany both could not register their places in the pre – QF stage.. Let's feel the 15 matches of this part through their highlights:

31. Match No 31

    Played between Brazil (world ranking 1) and Switzerland (world ranking 15), Brazil got the better of Switzerland by the margin of 1-0, confirming its place in the pre – QF round. Although Switzerland is a much inferior team than Neymar's (Jr) mighty Brazil, it gave a tough time for the latter.

32. Match No 32

    This match saw Portugal (ranking 9) taking on Uruguay (ranking 14). Uruguay also gave Portugal its tough time when it held up Portugal for the first 85' of the game. However, Portugal came back strongly by scoring 2 goals in the last 5' of the game. What a thrilling match!

33. Match No 33

Comparatively, the two weak teams of the tournament, Ecuador (ranking 44) and Senegal (ranking 18) put up a lazy show, in which Senegal beat Ecuador by 2-1 and booked its place in pre – QF stage.

34. Match No 34

The host Qatar (ranking 50) locked horn with world No 8, The Netherlands and as expected, the Dutch showed Qatar the way to ouster from the tournament by defeating them with a score of 2- O.

35. Match No 35

Played between Iran(ranking 20) and the USA (ranking 16), the duo having almost similar Soccer skills, USA blanked Iran by 1-0 to book its place in pre – QF after a long gap of 16 years.

36. Match No 36

It was played between two new neighbors, namely Britain (ranking 5) and New South Wales (ranking 19), the former members of the same conglomerate. Bruisers comfortably defeated Wales by 3-0 to enter the pre – QF stage. The first timer in the World Cup, Wales finished their journey of the World Cup and got boarded out from the pre-QF race.

37. Match No 37

Defending champion France (ranking 4) and Tunisia (ranking 30) played this match (in fact mismatch) in which, to an utter surprise, Tunisia stunned France as well as the Soccer lovers when it defeated France by 1-0 creating one of the biggest upsets of the tournament. Tunisian Wahbi Khazri, a midfielder, scored the lone goal in the 58′ of the game which appeared to be a goalless match till then. However, Tunisia got out of the tournament while France entered the pre – QF stage.

38. Match No 38

Teams Australia (ranking 38) and Denmark (ranking 10) had a very close match in which Australia got an edge when it toppled tenth-rank Denmark to win the match by 1-0. After a goalless first half, Denmark attacked the Aussies goal -post with a number of clever moves by its forwards but in vain. The only goal by Australia came in 82′, making Aussies the winner. Australian defense could not be penetrated by Denmark's stickers in the last minutes of the game, thus paving the way for Australia to enter the pre-QF stage leaving behind the better-ranked Denmark.

39. Match No 39

This match between the two strong sides, Messi's Argentina (ranking 3) and Poland (ranking 26) marked the beginning of the December phase of the tournament in which Argentina conveniently defeated Polish by 2-0. Argentina's victory was a must for them to enter pre -QF as they had already lost their opening encounter with rookie Saudi Arabia by 2-1. The two goals posted by Argentina were respectively in the 79th and 85th minutes of the game.

40. Match No 40

The match between two lukewarm teams, namely Saudi Arabia (ranking 51) and Mexico (ranking 13), in which Mexico needed the victory at least by 2 goals without getting goaled. Although this pressure on Mexican footballers was nicely taken they could not stop SA from scoring a goal on them in the additional time and in spite of Mexico winning the match by 2-1, Mexico had to say goodbye to the WC due to the complex technicality of the game. The gainer of this situation was Poland which entered the pre -QF stage.

41. Match No 41

A victory for Belgium (ranking 2) was important for Belgium to enter the pre -QF stage but due to a brave show by Croatian (ranking 12) players, the match went goalless. On this basis, Belgium went out of the tournament after 32 years in the history of the WC.

42. Match No 42

Played between Canada (ranking 41) and Morocco (22), this match saw Morocco defeat Canada by 2-1, making Morocco enter pre -QF stage for the first time. The last time Morocco entered the pre -QF was way back in the 1978 -edition of the WC. (At that time Morocco used to play by the name Republic of Morocco). Morocco became only the second country from the Gulf after UAE (2002) to enter the pre -QF stage.

43. Match No 43

In this match, Spain (ranking 7) and Japan (ranking 24) clashed for entering the pre -QF stage, and the match was won by low-ranked Japan by 2-1, thus Japan entered the next stage of pre – QF. The last time Japan entered the pre – QF stage was in 2010. On the other hand, Spain's entry in pre -QF became dependent on the outcome of the next match between Germany and Costa Rica.

44. Match No 44

This match between Germany (ranking 11) and Costa Rica (ranking 31) was important not only for its winner to move ahead but also for Spain for the same reason. The pre-condition for Germans was to score at least 5 goals and not to concede more than one goal. In the finally ended match of 100 minutes with 2 extended times, Germany's fate was sealed when they could win the match only by 4-2. This way both Germany and Costa Rica were out of the tournament and Spain entered the pre – QF stage.

45. Match No 45

South Korea (ranking 28) and Portugal (ranking 9) locked horns and the result went in the favor of SK by 2-1. Thus SK moved onto the pre -QF stage whereas Portugal's fate was to be decided in the next match between Ghana and Uruguay.

Footballers of the World–4: FIFA World Cup 2022

Readers, in this part of the 5 – series articles, we present to you the highlights of matches 46 to 60 played between December 2 and December 11 in the FIFA World Cup 2022 in Qatar.

This article comprises glimpses of the last 3 Prelim round matches (out of 48), all 8 matches of pre -QF stage, and all 4 matches of the QF – stage.

In the 3 Prelim – round matches, Soccer - great Brazil (match no 48) moved ahead to enter the pre – QF stage but another biggie of soccer – Uruguay (match no 46) crashed out of the tournament after losing its match against Ghana. Match no 47 of the Prelim round played between Switzerland

and Serbia and won by Switzerland was merely a formal one as Switzerland had qualified for the next round and Serbia was already out of the race of pre – QF stage.

In all the 8 matches of pre -QF, the match between Morocco and 2010- World Cup holder Spain will be remembered for a long due to Spain getting out of the tournament at the hands of a comparatively much weaker team Morocco. The match was decided in the Penalty shoot-out as the game was tied.

The biggest upset of the tournament took place in the QF – the stage when 5 -the times WC holding team Brazil was shown the door by the finalist of 2018 – WC edition Croatia (match no 57) when they defeated Brazil in the Penalty shootout. France, the defending champion of the WC became the first team to enter the semi-final stage. Morocco, Argentina, and Croatia are the other 3 semi-finalists of this year's FIFA.

Significantly, Morocco became the first-ever African team to qualify for the semi-final.

In the following lines, let us feel the furor of all 15 matches of this part of the article.

46. Match no 46

    This group H match was played between one-time WC champion Uruguay and Ghana. In the opinion of all the soccer-following sports lovers, the apparent winner was Uruguay but to the utter surprise of everyone, Ghana did a miracle by beating Uruguay by 2-0 and created another upset in the tournament. After the exit from Uruguay, South Korea got an opportunity to enter the pre – QF stage by sheer luck.

47. Match no 47

    In a close encounter between Switzerland and Serbia, it was the fighting spirit of Switzerland that made them enter the pre-QF. The victory came in the extra time of the match when Freueler placed the ball into Serbia's post to turn the final score to 3-2. With this victory, Switzerland became the last team to enter the pre -QF stage.

48. Match no 48

    In this last match of the prelim round played between Brazil and Cameroon, the latter stunned mighty Brazil when it unexpectedly defeated them by 1-0. However, Brazil had already qualified for the QF round of the tournament. This defeat of the king of football, Brazil, was their first defeat in FIFA by any African nation.

49. Match no 49

    This match marked the beginning of pre -QF (round of 16) stage. Played between Holland and USA, the match was won by Holland 3-1

    Making Holland become the first team to enter the QF – stage.

50. Match no 50

    The Soccer -great Messi's Argentina defeated Australia by 2-1 and announced its entry into the QF stage, knocking Aussies out of the tournament. It was Argentina's

6th consecutive entry into the QF stage. The winning goal was posted by Messi in the 88th minute of the otherwise match heading for a tie of 1-1.

51. Match no 51

Defending champion France stormed into the QF stage after defeating Poland by 3-1 in a straight encounter, where all 4 goals were made through field goals.

52. Match no 52

In this match, England crushed the otherwise known giant-killer Senegal by 3-0 to enter the QF -stage in style.

53. Match no 53

After getting tied by 1-1, the match saw Croatia Entering into the QF -stage through a Penalty shootout after defeating Japan by 3-1. This was the first match of QF -stage of this year's WC getting decided by 5 Penalties granted to both of the teams. Team Japan which got the distinction of knocking Soccer -biggies Germany and

Spain out of this year's WC, thus made its ouster from the WC.

54. Match no 54

The match saw Brazil showing the door to the lucky – to- enter pre -QF stage team South Korea by 4-1 and thus the most fancied team Brazil stormed into the QF – stage of WC. All the goals were through field goals. The dominance of Brazil in this match was such that it held the possession of the ball for 78 % of playing time, leaving only 22% for helpless SK.

55. Match no 55

The second – the last match of the knockout stage was won surprisingly won by Morocco defeating one-time WC champion Spain on a penalty shoot-out the basis by 3-0. Thus Morocco became the first African nation to enter the QF – stage of WC.

56. Match no 56

The match between Portugal and Switzerland became a pleasure to watch as the number of goals was posted in this match.

The one-sided match was won by Portugal by 6-1 making its way to the QF stage.

57. Match no 57

The first QF was between Brazil and Croatia, in which 5-time champion Brazil was up against Croatia, a team not known to be a great footballing nation. The match began with the highest number of spectators, Brazil being the favorite of the majority of them. Croatia played their heart out and prevented Brazil from scoring a single goal till 87 'of breath-stopping

Football. In the 88th 'of the game, Brazil scored the first goal which was equalized by Croatia in the 98' of the game. The match went without any result even after the completion of all the permissible extra timings, it was finally decided based on a Penalty shootout. Croatia won the match by 4-2, to move into the Semi-final of the WC for the 4th consecutive time.

Brazil's ouster from the game was one of the stunning outcomes of this WC. Brazil missed reaching the SF four 4 consecutive times.

58. Match no 58

Played between two top contenders of the WC Holland and Argentina, 1-1 was the score after the completion of the first half. At the finish of the full 90′ of the game, the match was squared at 2-2. When there was no result even after the completion of 130' of superb excitement, the match was decided based on a Penalty shootout, in which Argentina defeated Holland by 4-2. Argentina made its way to SF, outstaring 4- time WC champion The Netherlands.

59. Match no 59

In the third QF match, Portugal locked horns with the new entrant Morocco. Morocco could stop Portugal from taking a lead in the first half despite some good advances by the great footballer Cristiano Ronaldo. For the next 40′ of the second half, the match was again heading for a draw but with a superb goal of Cheddira of Morocco in the 86′, Morocco became the next semifinalist of the WC.

60. Match no 60

In the last QF match between France and England, the only unbeaten team San Morocco in this WC, England took a lead of 1-0 only in the 13′ of the game but France equalized it in the 71′ of the game. In the last minute of the game, France did a miracle and scored the winning goal, sending heartbroken England out of the game. With this match, all 4 semi-finalists Argentina, Croatia, France, and Morocco will gear up for winning the prestigious WC, in 2022.

Footballers of the World–5: FIFA World Cup 2022

In this part of a series of articles, we are putting forward the description of the culmination of the FIFA World Cup, which lasted for 29 days. This write-up describes the Final, the memorable moments of the tournament, the top achievers, and the glittering closing ceremony. We have also outlined two new features of FIFA, 2026.

THE ROAD TO THE FINALE

The two teams which entered the Final of the tournament were decided after 60 rounds of grueling clashes between 32 nations. The two teams were France and Argentina. Before the grand finale, the two semi-finals which decided the finalists, and the match held for the third place also enthralled soccer lovers.

In the first SF, Argentina and Croatia locked horns with each other while in the second SF, the defending champion France took on giant killer Morocco. In the Argentina – Croatia match, Argentina was the favorite and with the two nicely made moves of Messi in the 33rd and 61st minutes, Argentina proved its supremacy over Croatia and won the first SF by 3 -0. This was Argentina's 6th entry into the finals. In the second SF, France kept away the advances of Morocco and avoided any more upset by the Moroccans. France won the match by 2-0 to enter the Final for the 7th time to take on mighty Argentina. The losers of the two SFs, Croatia and Morocco faced each other for the 3rd place in which Croatia comfortably overcome Moroccans by 2-1.

THE FINAL

Much awaited final of the grand soccer event was held between Messi's Argentina and Mbappe's France in which France surprised everyone with its disappointing and slow moves in the first half of the game, which fetched two goals for Argentina. In the second half, France somehow woke up from slumber and put some life into the game when Mbappe scored two continuous goals to stun the viewers. But it was Argentinian day who turned the match in their favor to win it by 4-2 in the penalty shootout after a long marathon of 120 minutes of the total game time. This was their 3rd World Cup after a long wait of 36 years.

MEMORABLE MOMENTS

This year's FIFA had some exceptional moments which are:

1. Super soccer giant Brazil got defeated by a weaker team Cameroon in the group stage
2. Two top – most world cup contenders, Belgium and Germany got qualified for the tournament only in the Preliminary stage,
3. Good gestures were shown by Japanese fans during the matches Japan. Fans used to clean the stadium before every match against Japan, holding posters such as Save Environment.

4. Excellent examples of true sportsman spirit were shown by Team Wales against Team Iran in spite of the issuance of a yellow card to Iranian player Al Habibi, Wales did not challenge his substitution. Habibi, later on, played a match-winning game.

5. FIFA allowed wives/girlfriends of the players to wear the same numbered jerseys as those of their playing husbands/ boyfriends.

TOP ACHIEVERS

Player of the tournament (Golden ball) was given to Argentina's Messy for their all-around display of Soccer skills in the game and the Golden boot was given to Mbappe for hitting the maximum number (8) of goals. The best goalkeeper award went also to Argentina.

In the next edition of 2026, the tournament will have 12 groups, each containing 3 teams. Also, 3 countries USA, Canada, and Mexico will jointly host the next edition instead of one.

THE CLOSING CEREMONY

The mega event of 29 breath- stopping game with its theme song "Hayya Hayya" (meaning in English, "being together in all the times") came to an end with the glittering performances of artists taken from different parts of the globe including our own Nora Fatehi. The closing ceremony was truly named "the wonderful world".

The writer expresses his gratitude towards the Editor for having published this series of 5 articles on FIFA.

India's Convenient Win over Sri Lanka

After two disappointing defeats of team India in the World Cup and the Asia Cup held in September and October 2022, BCCI handed over the reins of the T20 I series against Sri Lanka held recently on January 3, 5, and 7 to the last year's IPL- hero and dynamic youngster Hardik Pandya and a fully new squad having young cricketers. For the first time, there were no senior legendary players including Rohit Hitman Sharma and Virat Kohli in the team.

In the first encounter held at Wankhede stadium, Mumbai on January 3, young India started its journey with a win. Although in the second match of 3- the match series held at MCA Stadium, Pune, team India lost by 16 runs and the series stood at 1-1, the determined and energetic team India annihilated Sri Lankan Tigers by a big margin of 91 runs in the series decider held at Rajkot to clinch the series by 2-1. Let's have closer look at the highlights of the 3 matches.

First T20 I

Held at Mumbai, India set a target of 163 runs for Sri Lanka in the allotted 20 overs. India's opening pair Kishen and Gill could not survive beyond 2.3 overs when Gill was superbly dismissed by carom ball spinner Theekshana at a meager score of 7 when India's score was 27/1. One down SKY, who is elevated as Vice-Captain, took charge in place of Gill but shocked everyone with his untimely careless high-rise shot and went back to dug out at a score of 7 when India's score was 38/2. Samson(5),

Kishen (37) and Skipper Pandya (29) also could not face the smart bowling changes by Sri Lanka's skipper Shanaka and left Team India lurching at 94/5 in 14.1 overs. The 68 -runs partnership between Axar Patel and Deepak Hooda in the remaining 5.5 overs guided India to a respectable total of 162 runs. In its reply, Sri Lanka too had a poor start and scored 24/2. The new bee Shivam Mavi (4/22) supported by Jammu Express Umran Malik(2/27) and Harshal Patel (2/41) wrapped up Sri Lanka's inning when it was 2 runs behind the Indian total. Thus India's young brigade won the opening match by 2 runs and took a lead of 1-0 in the series.

Second T20 I

Held in the cultural capital of Maharashtra, Pune on January 5, Indian Skipper Pandya won the toss and invited Sri Lanka to bat first. Playing carefully for squaring the series, Sri Lanka amassed a big total of 206/6 in 20 overs for Team India to chase 207 runs for a win. But, as in the first T20 I, the opening pair of Kishen (2)and Gill(5) once again could not put up a good total and India's total was 21/2 with the help of 10 extra runs. Except for a smashing inning of SKY (51 off 36 balls) and Axar Patel (65 off 31 balls), the rest of the batters fell prey to Sri Lanka's mediocre bowling and India lost the match by 16 runs.

The series was now open at 1-1. And every cricket lover was anxiously waiting for the series decider.

Third T20 I

Held in Rajkot on January 5, India batted first. It was the inning of SKY, who mesmerized the audience as well as the Sri Lankan team with his 112* off just 51 balls with 7 boundaries and 9 sixes to pile up the Indian Score at 228/5. Tripathi (35 off 16), Gill (46 off 36), and Axar (21*off 9) gave good support to make India reach the mammoth total of 228/5.

Not much was left for Indian bowlers, who finished the match when Sri Lanka's total was 137, all out in 20 overs. Indian bowlers Arshdeep Singh (3/20 off 2.4 overs), Pandya (2/30 off 4 overs), Chahal (2/30 off 3 overs) and Malik (2/31 off 3 overs) did all the damage with their disciplined bowling and gave Team India its series win by 2-1. In this match, SKY was not the limit for 'SKY'.

Deepanshu Srivastava

www.ingramcontent.com/pod-product-compliance
Lightning Source LLC
La Vergne TN
LVHW041155150826
845673LV00001B/164

* 9 7 9 8 8 9 1 3 3 6 8 4 1 *